KU-547-047

PET

AKWAEKE EMEZI

90 YEARS OF EXCELLENCE

FABER & FABER

CHAPTER 1

There shouldn't be any monsters left in Lucille.

The city used to have them, of course—what city didn't? They used to be everywhere, thick in the air and offices, in the streets and in people's own homes. They used to be the police and teachers and judges and even the mayor; yeah, the mayor used to be a monster. Lucille has a different mayor now. This mayor is an angel; the last couple of mayors have all been angels. Not like a from-heaven, not-quite-real type of angel but a from-behind-and-inside-and-in-front-of-the-revolution, therefore-very-real type of angel.

It was the angels who took apart the prisons and the police; who held councils prosecuting the former officers who'd shot children and murdered people, sentencing them to restitution and rehabilitation. Many people thought it wasn't enough; but the angels were only human, and it's hard to build a new world without making people angry. You try your best, you move with compassion, you think about the big structures. No revolution is perfect. In the meantime, the angels banned firearms, not just because of the school shootings but also because of the kids who shot themselves and their families at home; the civilians who thought they could shoot people who didn't look like them, just because they got mad or scared or whatever, and nothing would happen to them because the old law liked them better than the dead. The angels took the laws and changed them, tore down those horrible statues of rich men who'd owned people and fought to keep owning people. The angels believed and the people agreed that there was a good amount of proper and deserved shame in history and some things were just never going to be things to be proud of.

Instead, they put up other monuments. Some were statues of the dead, mostly the children whose hashtags had been turned into battle cries during the revolution. Others were giant sculptures with thousands of names carved into them, because too many people had died and if you made statues of everyone, Lucille would be filled with stone figures and there'd be no room for the alive ones. The names were of people who died when the hurricanes hit and the monsters wouldn't evacuate the prisons or send aid, people who died when the monsters sent drones and bombs to their countries (because, as the angels pointed out, you shouldn't use a nation as a basis to choose which deaths you mourn; nations aren't even real), people who died because the monsters took away their health care—names and names of people and people, countless letters recording that they had been.

The citizens of Lucille put dozens of white candles at the base of each monument, hung layers of marigold necklaces around the necks of the statues, and, when they walked past, would often fall silent for a moment and press a palm against the stone, soaking up the heat the sun had left in it, remembering the souls the stone was holding. They'd remember the marches and vigils, the shaky footage that was splashed everywhere of their deaths (a thing that wasn't allowed anymore, that gruesome dissemination of someone's child gasping in their final moments, bubbling air or blood or grief—the angels respected the dead and their loved ones). The people of Lucille would remember the temples that were bombed, the mosques, the acid attacks, the synagogues. Remembering was important.

Jam was born after the monsters, born and raised in Lucille, but like everyone else, she remembered. It was taught in school: how the monsters had maintained power for such a long time; how the angels had removed them, making Lucille what it is today. It wasn't like the angels wanted to be painted as heroes, but the teachers wanted the kids to *want* to be angels, you see? Angels could change the world, and Lucille was proof. Jam was fascinated by them, by the stories

3

the teachers told in history class. They briefly mentioned other angels, those who weren't human, but only to say that Lucille's angels had been named after these other ones. When Jam asked for more information, her teachers' eyes slid away. They mentioned religious books, but with reluctance, not wanting to influence the children. Religion had caused so many problems before the revolution, people were hesitant to talk about it now. "If you really want to know," one of the teachers added, taking pity on Jam's frustrated curiosity, "there's always the library."

Why can't they just tell me? Jam complained to her best friend, Redemption, as they left the school. Her hands were a blur as she signed, and Redemption smiled at her annoyance. It was the last day of classes before summer break, and while he was excited to do nothing for the next several weeks except train, Jam was—as always—on some hunt for information.

"You're giving yourself homework," he pointed out.

Aren't you curious? she replied. *Who the old angels were, if they weren't human?*

"If they were even real, you mean." Redemption adjusted the strap of his backpack. "You know that's what a lot of religion was, right? Just made-up things used to scare people so they could control us better."

Jam frowned. *Maybe,* she said, *but I still wanna know.*

Redemption threw an arm around her. "And you wouldn't be you if you didn't," he laughed. "I gotta go pick up the lil bro from his class and walk him home, but let me know what you find out, okay?"

Okay. She hugged him goodbye. *Give Moss a kiss for me.*

He scoffed. "I'll try, but that boy thinks he grown now."

Too grown for kisses??

"That's what *I* said." Redemption threw up his hands as he headed off. "Talk soon, love you!"

Love you! Jam waved goodbye and watched him break into a jog, his body moving with an easy grace, then she went to the library to look up pictures of angels.

The librarian was a tall, dark-skinned man who whizzed around the marble floors in his wheelchair. His name was Ube, and Jam had known him since she was a toddler pawing through picture books. She loved being in the library, the almost sacred silence you could find there, the way it felt like another home. Ube smiled at her when she walked in, and Jam took an index card from his counter, writing her question about angels down on it. She slid it over to Ube, and he grunted as he read it, nodding his head, then he wrote some reference numbers underneath her question and slid the card back to her. They didn't need to talk, which was perfect.

It took her fifteen minutes to find the old pictures, printed on thin, flaky paper and nestled between heavy book covers. Even though Ube hadn't said she should, Jam considered pulling on the white gloves nestled in the reading desk drawers to use in looking through the books, they seemed that old. But they weren't in the protected section, so she figured it was fine to run her bare fingers over the smooth and fragile paper. The room she was in was quiet, with large windows vaulting up the walls and domed skylights pouring in late-afternoon sun. Jam sat for a few minutes with her fingers on the images, staring down, turning a page, and staring at the next one. They were strong and confusing pictures. Eventually she closed and stacked the books, then lugged them to the checkout counter.

Ube raised a thick black eyebrow at her. "All of these?" he asked. His voice sounded unreal, deep and velvet, something that should live only in a radio because it didn't make sense outside in normal air.

Jam nodded.

"You gotta be careful with them, you know? They're mad old."

She nodded again, and Ube looked at her for a moment, then smiled, shaking his head.

"You right, you a careful girl. Always seen it." He scanned the books as he spoke. "You treat the books gentle, like they flowers or something."

She blushed.

"Don't be shy about it, now. Books are important." He stamped them for her. "You need a bag, baby?"

Jam shook her head no.

"All right, now. Two weeks, remember?"

She hefted the books onto her hip, nodded, and left. They were a weight straining against her arm until she got home, and she took them straight upstairs to her mother's studio. Jam's mother had been born when there were monsters, and Jam's grandmother had come from the islands, a woman entirely too gentle for that time. It had hurt her too much to be alive then, hurt even more to give birth to Jam's mother, whose existence was the result of a monster's monstering. This grandmother had died soon after the birth, but not before naming Jam's mother Bitter. No one had argued with the dying woman.

Bitter knew her name was heavy, but she hadn't minded, because it was honest. That was something she'd taught Jam—that a lot of things were manageable as long as they were honest. You could see things clearly if they were honest; you could decide what to do next, because you knew exactly what you were dealing with. She never lied to Jam, always told her the truth, even if sometimes she couldn't make it as gentle as she would've wanted, for her daughter's sake. But Jam trusted her mother for those brutal truths, and that's why home was the first place she brought the books with the angels in them.

Her mother was painting when Jam came in, so the studio was full of loud music, old-school grime this time, the energy thumping against the light and Stormzy's voice whipping around Bitter's flying braids. Jam put the books down on a table that wasn't too crowded and leaned her elbows on them, watching her mother's shoulder blades jerk and convulse as she moved on her hands and knees, a massive canvas stretched beneath her. Bitter was clutching a brush between her fingers, her joints locked in angles that looked painful, her eyes partially closed and her mouth slightly open. She always painted like this, half dancing in something of a trance, and she was always exhausted afterward. Jam didn't want to interrupt her.

Jam's father, Aloe, was the one who was good at getting through to his wife when she was working. It was something about his vibe, Jam thought, something about how attuned they were to each other. All Aloe had to do was be close enough to Bitter. He'd crouch a few feet away from the edge of her canvas and just wait, breathing as he always did, steady and calm. Jam had watched it many times—the way her mother's hands would slow down, the brushstrokes growing softer, shorter, and eventually how Bitter would stop moving altogether, her shoulders settling like a bird landing and folding in its wings. Her long neck would curve back, raising her face, and she'd look straight at Aloe, and her smile would be like a whole new day starting.

Jam crawled under the table and curled up on a blanket that had been left there. It was getting harder to fit into these small spaces she liked to hide in; her arms and legs were getting longer from her growth spurts, and she was almost as tall as Bitter now. Her ankles flopped against the hardwood, and she bent her arms into a pillow under her head and slept, the bass from the music drumming into her bones through the floor. It felt like only a few minutes before her mother's hand drifted against her cheek.

"Jam-jam? Wake up, sweetness."

She blinked and Bitter's face came into focus, a piece at a time, the hard cheekbones, the bare eyebrows, the broad mouth pressed with a matte red. Her mother's teeth spread into view as she smiled at Jam, sharp and white. The music had stopped. "Welcome back, child," Bitter said. "Stand up?"

Jam took her mother's hand and pulled herself out, avoiding the edge of the table. She'd knocked her head against it too many times before.

"How long you been under there for?"

Jam shrugged and her mother brushed imaginary dirt off her hair. Bitter's face was smudged with a couple of different white paints: a bright white that seemed holy; a duller, slightly yellowed ivory, as if a magical tusk had touched her forehead; a cream trailing dry and broken down her neck.

"Painting?" Jam asked. Bitter was one of the few people she voiced with.

"Come see." They walked over and Jam leaned forward to look at the painting. It was manywhite and thick and textured, paint climbing on itself as if it wanted to get away from the canvas, away from the floor underneath the canvas, even. There were raked gouges in it, next to delicate veined imprints, next to pieces of Bitter's palm. Something large and loud in the center of the painting had the hind legs of a goat, fur like grated bone, solid thighs, their surface thrusting toward the ceiling of the studio. Jam pointed at it and looked at her mother. Bitter held her chin, thoughtful.

"I'm not sure, you know. The thing just coming out the way it want so."

Its arms were long, even longer than Jam's. It didn't have a head yet. The smoke Bitter had painted around it was as dense as clouds, and Jam thought she could see it move, a jerky tendril here and there.

"Name?" she asked.

Bitter shrugged. "You could name something when you not sure what it is?" They stood and looked down together at the thing struggling out of smoke. "It's just waiting sometimes," Bitter murmured. "Just waiting." Jam wasn't sure if she meant that she was waiting for the thing to show itself or if the thing itself was waiting for Bitter to be done making it. Maybe they were one and the same. She took her mother's hand and pulled her toward the angel books.

"Ah," said Bitter. "What you have there?" Jam flipped some of the books open to the pages where she'd tucked the glittered bookmarks Redemption gave her on her last birthday. She pushed the books out across the table so her mother could see the pictures in each of them.

They were supposed to be angels, but they were terrifying: eyes filled with licking flames even as they looked out from the page, armored faces that weren't faces, wings full of mouths, wheels of reddened eyes, four-headed forms that weren't even vaguely human. There was a butchered lion head bleeding somewhere in there. Bitter hummed and touched the pictures.

Jam looked up at her. "Angels?"

Bitter hummed some more and nodded.

Jam frowned. *But Lucille, the mayor and the council and everyone who came together to take away the monsters, those were angels, not these,* she signed.

Her mother ran her stained fingers across the books. "'Do not be afraid,'" she said.

Jam didn't understand, so she kept the frown on her face.

"That's the first thing angels does say, you know? Do not be afraid."

Jam looked down at the pictures. It seemed like a reasonable opening line, considering how horrific they looked. Her mother laughed at her expression.

"Exactly," she said. "We does think angels are white robes and harps and all kinds of pretty things, but chile!" She clicked her tongue. "Look at them. Good reason why they does strike fear into the heart."

Jam wondered—if real angels looked like this, then what did that mean for the angels in Lucille? Did it mean people didn't really know what they were talking about when they said angels in the first place? Angels weren't supposed to look like this. They were supposed to be good, and how could something good look like this?

She tapped on the pictures and looked up at her mother, worried, pitching her voice low. "Monsters," she whispered.

Bitter's eyebrows shot up. "You think so?" She hummed some more and turned a few of the pages. "Well, I suppose one could see how you could see that. Only if you don't know what a monster looks like, of course."

What does a monster look like? Jam asked.

Her mother focused on her, cupping her cheek in a chalky hand. "Monsters don't look like anything, doux-doux. That's the whole point. That's the whole problem."

Okay, Jam thought, fine. She wasn't worried about the monsters anyway; she was worried about Lucille's angels, because if they secretly looked like the pictures, then it was hard to imagine that they hadn't done, well, some pretty bad things.

Our angels, she signed, *the ones here. Are they good? Are they innocent?*

Angels had to be innocent, right? Wasn't that the whole point of them, to be good and innocent and righteous?

Bitter tilted her head, and something sad entered her eyes. "It not easy to get rid of monsters," she said. "The angels, they had to do things underhand, dark things." The sadness in her eyes deepened, and Jam took her hand, not understanding what pain was coming up but feeling its ripples in the air. "Hard things," her mother continued. "You can't sweet-talk a monster into anything else, when all it does want is monsterness. Good and innocent, they not the same thing; they don't wear the same face."

She came back to herself and studied Jam for a little bit, the sadness lifting from her eyes. "It's good to think about the angels like so," she said. "Critically, yes? Can't believe everything everyone tells you, even in school, it's good to question. But remember, is Lucille angels that organized we. And what did we learn from that?" Bitter squeezed Jam's hands. "Tell it to me."

Jam made a face.

"You don't have to voice it, you could sign it, ent?"

Jam sighed and freed her hands from her mother's so she could say the words, lifted from an old Gwendolyn Brooks poem, words the angels had used when they gave Lucille back to itself. A revolution cry.

We are each other's harvest. We are each other's business. We are each other's magnitude and bond.

"Yes, child. Angels aren't pretty pictures in old holy books, just like monsters aren't ugly pictures. It's all just people, doing hard things or doing bad things. But is all just people, our people."

Jam thought about that. So pictures could be wrong—wait, no. She'd seen too much of her mother's work to think *that* simply. Pictures could be flat-out lies, yes, but what she was really thinking was that pictures could be misleading. That made more sense, more trickster sense, showing your eyes one thing and tripping your feet in another direction. Like stories. And besides, she would trust anything her mother had to say about monsters. She knew about her grandfather, the monster that caught her grandmother. If there was anyone who knew what a monster was or was not, it would be Bitter, the daughter of one.

Her mother reached out and touched her chin. "Matter fix, doux-doux?"

Jam nodded shyly and smiled. Bitter leaned forward and kissed her forehead just as they heard the front door open.

"And look, your father home already."

True enough, Aloe's voice boomed through the house. "Where are my girls?" he shouted.

Bitter ruffled Jam's hair and stood up to gather and clean her brushes. "Studio, darling!" she yelled back, and they heard Aloe's feet crash up the stairs. Bitter often joked to Jam that her father moved like a functioning disaster, clumsy and charming and breaking at least one breakable thing a week. He was tall and broad, and he filled up the doorway for a heartbeat when he entered, his face splitting into a smile to see them. Jam always felt lucky when she stood in the path of her father's joy. He was shrugging off his jacket, and his chest was expansive under it—"I was built to be a local farmer back home on the continent," he always said, but he'd gone another way and ended up as a paramedic. He liked the adrenaline of saving people. He always wanted to protect them, make it better. It made him good at his job, better as a father. When Jam was a toddler, she'd refused to speak, which was why they'd taught her to sign instead. She used her hands and body and face for her words but saved her voice for the most important one—screamed out during her first and only temper tantrum, when she was three, when someone had complimented her for the thousandth time by calling her "such a handsome little boy" and Jam had flung herself on the floor under her parents' shocked gazes, screaming her first word with explosive sureness.

"Girl! Girl! Girl!"

Bitter had stared before laughing. "All right, sweetness," she'd said, looking at the writhing child and thinking back on several arguments they'd had about Jam's clothes, when Jam would sign refusal over and over. "That explains that."

Aloe had shaken his head and picked his daughter up, locking her flailing limbs against his body. "Sorry, sorry," he'd murmured against her head. "Ewela iwe, eh? We didn't know." He'd patted her head until she calmed down, and then they took her home and Aloe started researching puberty blockers and the hormones she might need. Protecting his daughter was a life mission he remained dedicated to. When she was ten, Jam got an implant with the blockers, and it was a few years of vitamins and regular bone scans before she swapped it out at thirteen for a hormone implant, a tiny cylinder nestled in her upper arm, administering estrogen to her body. Jam watched her body change with delight, the way her hips widened, how her breasts were growing. She would poke at them, swiveling in the mirror to see them from every angle, running her hands down her new body. Bitter laughed, then taught her how to do breast self-exams and talked to her about fertility options.

Jam was fifteen when she told Aloe she wanted surgery, and her father sat and wrapped his arms around her.

"You know you're still a girl whether you get surgery or not, right? No one gets to tell you anything different."

Jam had smiled at him, almost taller than he was. *I know, Dad.* She wanted it anyway, and Aloe always gave his daughter what she wanted. It wasn't like how it used to be, back when the world was different for girls like her. She didn't have to wait to be considered an adult for her wants around her body to be acted on; her parents understood how important it was for her well-being.

After the surgery, Bitter painted a portrait of Jam reclining on their porch swing and wrapped in a blanket, her eyes tired but happy, her feet dangling in shimmering air. Less than a year later, the painting hung next to the door of the studio, and now Aloe leaned his hand on its frame as he took off his socks.

"How are you, darling?" he asked Jam.

She shrugged and closed her eyes as he pulled her into a hug, kissing the top of her head.

"She asking about angels and monsters and things," Bitter called over her shoulder, her voice a blend of amusement and pride. "Look at the books she brought."

17

Aloe glanced down and whistled. "That's very ugly." Jam giggled as he flipped a page. "What are you asking about them?"

Bitter wiped her brushes on a rag. "She asking if those angels are monsters, if Lucille angels are good."

"Ah, but we know how to handle any monsters we meet." Aloe tapped the pages with his left index and middle fingers. "Whether on the page or in life." He closed the books and stacked them carefully on top of each other before turning to Jam and holding her by the shoulders.

"We close them up, you hear? We lock them away."

"Aloe, we've talked about this," Bitter interjected. "Rehab centers not the same thing as prisons."

Aloe ignored her, focusing on Jam. "There are no monsters in Lucille," he said. He was radiating surety, wanting her to feel protected. Her father held more fear than her mother, Jam had always known this.

She raised her hands between them so he could see her sign, and he dropped his arms to give her space. *There are no free monsters in Lucille,* she corrected. She wanted to add *that we know of,* but she saw the fear pass through Aloe's eyes, a ghost glimmering across a room, so she let her hands stop. A minor sadness crept into his face, and he buried it in a smile.

"Don't grow up too quickly," he said.

Jam nodded and stepped back into his chest to hug him. His arms were live branches, growing around her. "Forget the monsters," he whispered.

They went to look at Bitter's unfinished painting, and Aloe could feel the thickness of it the same way Jam had. "It feels as if it's pushing itself up," he said, his voice soft with awe. He scratched his arm, discomfort pooling around him. "Nna mehn, Bitter. Are you sure this one doesn't want to become real?"

Bitter scoffed. Jam could feel a mild frustration in her, that the painting wasn't clear, that it was hiding around corners from her. She could hear her mother's thought quite distinctly, colored with some snark: the painting would have to know what it was before it could become real. Bitter always had contempt for undefined things, but only when she wanted them to be something else. Jam stifled a smile. It was nice to see how these conversations went between her mother and the work, this coy dance, this sufferhead behavior, as Aloe would say. Who told you to pick such a demanding discipline? he liked to tease. I didn't want to be lazy like you, Bitter would tease back. Jam watched Aloe kiss her mother, then the three of them went downstairs to make dinner together. But Aloe's words to Jam floated around in the studio air even after they'd left.

Forget the monsters.

He hadn't meant anything strong by it. Just to comfort his daughter, prompted by an old fear, by echoes of memories of what people used to do to girls like her. But an echo of a memory is not the same as a memory, and a memory is not the same as a now, and anyway, he'd said it loud enough that the painting heard it. Also, the problem is, when you think you've been without monsters for so long, sometimes you forget what they look like, what they sound like, no matter how much remembering your education urges you to do. It's not the same when the monsters are gone. You're only remembering shadows of them, stories that seem to be limited to the pages or screens you read them from. Flat and dull things. So, yes, people forget. But forgetting is dangerous.

Forgetting is how the monsters come back.

CHAPTER 2

It took Bitter three more weeks to finish the painting. She grew a new patience with it, like an extra skin. The music she used changed, softened. She was playing ragas now, haunting things full of sitar and tabla and sarod. She even closed the doors to the studio.

"Watching done for now," she said.

Aloe and Jam looked at each other and shrugged. What to do? They sat on the porch swing and ate bowls of home-made ice cream in the evenings while waiting for her to come down for dinner. More often than not, they ate alone together and then went to bed while the light from Bitter's studio stayed in the window like a glowworm. Sometimes Jam sat with her back against the studio door, her eyes closed and her palms flat on the floor. Aloe brought up her dinner, and when fatigue collided with her body and he found her curled up on her side, still pressed against the door, he slid a pillow under her head and draped a soft blanket over her.

When Bitter turned off the ragas and opened the door to see her daughter at her feet, she knelt and slid her arms under the girl, lifting her up. Jam's head fell against her mother's shoulder, and Bitter carried her to bed, even though Jam's weight wrenched at her back.

Bitter finished the painting in the dark morning of a day—it was well past midnight when Jam heard the studio door creak open. She stared into the velvet black of her room and listened to her mother's footsteps walking into her and Aloe's bedroom. There was a weight thrumming through the floorboards in a low song, and that was how Jam knew the painting was done. Bitter's feet were singing the news.

When her mother's feet were no longer touching the floor and things got quieter, Jam knew that Bitter was in bed, and so she swung her legs down and snuck out toward the studio. The air was as dark as pitch, but Jam knew every piece of their house whether she had eyes or not. At the studio door, she put her hand on the enamel doorknob. She was about to turn it and push the door open—she'd thought she was ready to do that—but all of a sudden, she became uncertain. The painting must be so fresh. Maybe it would be better to let it settle a little. Maybe it was too soon, it had just left her mother's hands, it seemed wrong to expose it to her own eyes without letting it have some time to itself. Just to exist, you know, just to be. Everyone, everything deserved some time to be. To figure out what they were. Even a painting. Bitter finishing it was just her telling it what she thought it was, or what she'd seen it as. It hadn't decided for itself yet. Jam didn't want to be rude, or inconsiderate, so she went back to bed.

Bitter left the studio alone for the next couple of days. It was the weekend when Jam finally decided to go and look at it, while her parents were out getting groceries. The studio door swung open and silent under her hand, surprising Jam. The creak was gone. Maybe the painting had eaten it.

Midday light was pouring through the large windows, and Jam could see that her mother had left the painting un-covered, flat on the floor. Even the last brushes she'd used on it were still there, the bristles stiffened with streaky red. Bitter hadn't cleaned them or put them away; she must have finished, dropped everything, and just walked out, which was strange. Bitter always cleaned her brushes. Jam went toward the painting, trying to keep her feet light, aware that she was basically trying to creep up on a canvas. It was so big, though, feet and feet of it on each side. At the edge of it, she leaned in.

Bitter had completed the figure in the middle, but it was nothing like what the softness of the ragas would have pre-dicted. The goat legs had stayed, jutting thighs and all, but from the waist up, the figure was new. A torso twisted all the way around, still furred, but the thick white was interrupted by a new bloodiness, intermittent streaks, as if the figure had made a mess while eating something. Or tearing something apart. The arms remained long, but they were feathered now, an iridescent gold ending in obscenely human hands. Photographs of Bitter's hands were strewn around as studies—she'd painted her own hands into the figure, painted crude stitches that grafted her wrists to its feathered arms. Jam shuddered; it was weird to see her mother's hands butchered like that. Bitter had painted the skin a brown that was stripped of any vibrance, so they looked dull and dead. Only the fingernails had color; they were metal claws the same gold as the feathers, as if some essence of the figure had pierced the mutilated flesh and burst out from the cuticles.

Jam's eyes traced up the arms and to the twisted torso, the arched back, the chest turned up to face the top of the painting. There were glints of silver in the splashed white of the chest, some metal her mother had embedded in the paint. The figure's head was heavy with curled ram's horns, clotted red, and the face was an interlocked geometric mess of metallic feathers that smothered any features. Only the shape of a mouth was visible, and it spewed the same smoke that filled the rest of the painting.

All of it scared Jam, way down into her bones. It was unlike anything her mother had ever painted before. It didn't feel good. Just looking at it made her feel dizzy, like the canvas was the only steady point in the world and everything else was slipping. Jam tried to straighten up, but her head was clogged and heavy and her toes hit the edge of the canvas and then she was falling, so slowly that it was floating, but she was falling onto the canvas. She threw out her hands to break the fall, and they landed on the figure's chest. One scraped across hardened paint, but the other became a slice of pain that cut through the dizziness. Jam gasped and scrambled backward off the painting until she was pushing away from it, her chest rough and heaving, her left palm loud with hurt. She glanced down and saw that it was bleeding.

What the—!

The blood spread across her lifeline, and Jam stared at the painting, at the small red drops she'd tracked along it, past the edge, onto the hardwood floor, bread crumbs leading to her.

Why on earth was she bleeding?

She got on her knees and shuffled back to the painting, peering at it without the vertigo of standing upright, cradling her hand to her chest. There were drops of her blood on the figure's chest where she'd fallen—though it was hard to tell them apart from the bloody streaks Bitter had already painted—and looking closer, she saw those glints of metal she'd noticed before. Jam tilted her head, and the light

25

danced off them, bright and steel. Her mouth fell open as she recognized what they were: razor blades. Oh shit, she thought. Bitter's gone mad.

Okay, maybe not entirely mad, but still. . . .

Her hand was stinging, and the blood had started dripping off her palm and onto her shirt. Jam got up quickly and left the studio, closing the door firmly behind her. She paused for a moment, wondering if she should have cleaned up the mess she'd made in there first, but the dampness spreading on her shirt reminded her how bad it would be if her parents came home to find her literally covered in blood. She needed to patch up this wound immediately so she could clean the studio before her blood dried completely into the floors— she'd never be able to hide it from Bitter then.

Aloe kept a comprehensive first aid kit in the house, accordioned shelves of supplies layered inside, and Jam dragged it out from under the bathroom sink. She stanched the bleeding with wadded paper towels, then pulled out alcohol wipes and a pack of butterfly closures. The cut was clean and deeper than she thought a plain Band-Aid could handle, than she would've thought a razor blade could cause. She made the torn edges kiss and held them together with the closures, then put a wide bandage over all of it. That way she could claim it was a scrape from falling off her bike. They wouldn't ask her too many questions. Every time Jam hurt herself around the house, Bitter shook her head ruefully and just said that Aloe's clumsiness had to have ended up somewhere. Jam shoved the kit back into its place and ran to her room, pulling her bloodied shirt off over her head. She pushed it to the bottom of her laundry basket and was pulling on a clean shirt when she heard the front door open.

Dammit, she thought. There wasn't enough time to go back into the studio. Maybe if she kept them downstairs during dinner?

"Jam? You home? Come help us with the bags," Aloe called, his voice carrying through the house.

"Coming!" she called back, to make sure he didn't come upstairs. She quickly flushed the reddened paper towels, hoping they wouldn't clog the toilet, then hurried down to the kitchen, pasting a smile over the anxiety she was feeling. Her parents didn't notice, and Jam stayed tense for the rest of the afternoon and into the evening, until halfway through dinner, when Aloe asked Bitter if she was going to work that night.

"I don't think so," Bitter replied. "Think I taking a little break, maybe another day or two."

Jam exhaled in relief, the tight knot of worry in her chest loosening a little but not entirely. When dinner was over and bedtime crawled in, Jam lay in her sheets waiting for her parents to fall asleep, properly asleep, before she could risk going back into the studio without waking them up. In the waiting, she fell asleep herself, startling awake only when she heard the floorboards singing a song she hadn't heard before. It was extraordinarily soft, barely a sound, even, but Jam knew it was there. She knew every sound the house made, and this was a new one, and it wasn't the house making it; this was just the house telling her. If it sounded like anything, it sounded like when you were boiling water and tiny bubbles started forming along the sides and bottom. The actual boiling hadn't begun yet, but it was the sound of a starting, and it was coming from the studio.

Jam opened her eyes and sat up, pulling off her bonnet. The sound continued. It didn't seem to be in a hurry, but it was steady. More importantly, there was no reason for the studio to be talking to the house unless Bitter was in it, so that alarmed Jam. She got out of bed and left her room, her palm throbbing. It took a moment before she noticed that the pulse in her palm was matching the song from the floor. That . . . couldn't be good. That meant something was happening with the painting, and that particular painting, out of everything Bitter had ever made, was the one piece that Jam definitely did not want anything like this to be happening with. Still, she crept toward the studio, because whatever was going on was probably her fault, after the whole sneaking-in-and-falling-down business, so hiding and waiting for someone else to deal with it in the morning wasn't an option. You took care of your own messes, her mom always said, plus she still had to clean up the blood.

The studio door opened without a sound, like it was conniving with her. Made sense, Jam thought. This felt personal, and in some ways the studio was an accomplice, or at the very least, a witness. She closed the door behind her even though she didn't think that her parents could hear the song—they didn't seem to listen to the house the way that she did.

The painting was a pool of moonlight in the center of the room. Jam's T-shirt stuck to her back, a cold sweat licking down her spine. She walked toward it, and the sound intensified. When she looked down at the painting, the smoke in the background was moving, churning and swirling. As she watched, it started lifting off the canvas, entering the air right above. Some part of her considered being scared, but the smoke was kind of beautiful, and besides, her mother had made it, so how could it hurt her? Even the feathers were moving now, in a fine tremble, moonlight pattering over the gold. Jam looked for her blood, expecting it to be old and dried by then, but her eyes found it easily because it was bright and pulsing and all the drops of it had migrated from the rest of the canvas, even from the floor, and it was all gathered on the figure's chest. The chalkfur Bitter had painted was rustling now, and Jam held back a cry as she saw the small blob of blood vanish into the painting with a quick sucking sound. She stumbled backward, her eyes wide, as the figure started coming out of the canvas.

Some small, rational part of her brain that wasn't screaming internally decided that none of this could actually be happening. Bitter was a wonderful painter, sure, but she wasn't that good, not turn-your-painting-into-some-kind-of-magic good. Unfortunately for rational Jam, the figure continued to blatantly prove her wrong, levering one arm out and reaching down to the floor for stability, the gold claws carving small strips from the hardwood. It pulled itself out chest first, then hefted its thighs out, hooves clattering on the floor. Smoke came with it, seemed to pour from it, in fact. The terror in Jam's chest paused at the sheer . . . awkwardness of the thing. It wasn't rising with grace so much as jerkily trying to extricate itself from the work, and its head was still buried in the canvas. It reminded Jam of once when Aloe was trying to fix a pipe in the basement but got his head stuck, and all he could do was wriggle and curse while Jam was laid out on the floor, laughing hysterically, until Bitter came down to see what the noise was about.

It was hard to be frightened of something that was straining to pop out its head like a cartoon. Jam wondered briefly if it needed some help; it really did seem to be just as clumsy as Aloe. Its hooves scrambled and slipped against the floor, and it fell down, its neck still pouring into the painting, and that was when Jam decided it couldn't be that dangerous. She didn't know if it could hear thoughts, and it definitely couldn't see signs, so she decided to voice, even though it might not hear that either, what with its head still stuck in there.

"Hold still," she said, coming up to it tentatively. Those claws were way bigger with the added dimension.

It stopped struggling when she spoke, and Jam reached down toward its shoulders, which were covered in the same sharp lines of metal feathers as its face. The feathers extended all the way down its back, and she stared at the patterns in awe. This was something from the other side of the painting, the parts Bitter's brushes hadn't touched. It was weird to see that they were real anyway. Jam wondered if it was the thing who got to decide what was on the other side, or if what was there had always just been there, or if Bitter's imagination had built it.

One of the thing's hands—her mother's hands—jerked, and the scrape of its claws dragged Jam's attention back. She grabbed its shoulders and pulled, but nothing happened.

A thought fed into her mind, and she recoiled because for the first time ever, at least so directly, it wasn't hers.

Do you think, it said with leaking contempt, that you possess more strength than I do, that you can just . . . pull me out?

Whoa, she thought back, letting go of its shoulders. Okay, that's weird.

There is no time for your astonishment, human, it snapped.

Jam folded her arms, feeling more defensive than scared. The silly thing couldn't even get out by itself. I'm just trying to help, she snapped back. Why you being so rude?

Merely pointing out facts, little girl, it countered. Now, pay attention. One of my horns is caught on something, so you need to get it loose.

Oh, so now you need my help, she started, then blinked down at the boiling smoke of the painting, distracted from her annoyance. Wait, what? You seriously want me to put my hand in there? Where does it even go?

The thing sighed and its voice dripped with even more condescension than it had before, which was kind of impressive. I wish, I truly wish, that I had the time to explain the intricacies of cross-dimensional portals to you, little girl, but I don't. Hurry up!

And just like that, she was back to being annoyed. Jam glared at the creature before realizing it couldn't actually see her, then resolved to pull the damn thing out just so she could glare at it properly. She took a deep breath and slid her hand into the painting, along the creature's neck, following the smooth metal of the feathers under her fingers.

It's the left horn, it told her, and Jam directed her hand that way. Inside, the painting felt like nothing. Just the cold and the smoke and the thing under her hand. The horn felt like regular horn when she got to it, until she traced along its length and felt a loop pressing down halfway. By now she'd reached into the painting almost up to her armpit.

I don't want to fall in, she warned.

You won't. The rest of the canvas is closed.

Jam felt around the loop that the horn was caught in. It was firm and cold, pulling the horn down, but if she wiggled her fingers underneath whatever it was made of—she was trying not to think too hard about that—she could push it forward a little, and that seemed to give a bit of room. The creature tried to pull up, and that crushed her fingers between the loop and the horn.

Ow, stop, stop! It did so immediately, but Jam still wanted to kick it, the careless thing. Push down, she told it, don't pull up! Down and then sideways. That should get you out.

It took a bit more wiggling to accommodate the spirals of the horn, but Jam felt it slip out and then felt the loop slither away, leaving a distinct residue of disappointment on her fingers. It was creepy to feel a feeling as if it was a substance, and Jam immediately yanked her arm out of the painting. She massaged it, trying to push out some of the numbness that had crawled in, trying to process that she'd just shoved a part of her body into—what?—another world. That was some weird shit. Jam looked at the creature, now free and sitting on the floor beside the empty canvas, surrounded by smoke and rubbing its horn. That was some other weird shit. Some seriously *other* other weird shit.

It glanced up at her with its nothing of a goldfeathered face and puffed some smoke out of its mouth.

Thank you, it said in her head, and Jam decided to ignore the grudging tone.

You're welcome, she replied, hoping it couldn't sense her returning fear. Um, what exactly are you?

Its chest fur rippled, and it tilted its head. Why don't you ask your mother? it deflected. She's the one who made me.

Jam frowned, not liking its reference to Bitter. Was there maybe a threat somewhere in there? Did it resent Bitter for painting it? She didn't know much about this strange, giant thing, but she didn't like how it was avoiding her question. It knew exactly what it was; it just didn't want to tell her.

Okay, then, she thought, then tell me why you're here? And don't lie to me.

The thing pulled in its legs and rose to a crouch. It was

almost seven feet tall, so even bent in half, it still looked terrifying.

I'm hunting.

The returning fear turned into a stampede in Jam's chest. She tried not to let it show. Um. O-kay. What . . . what do you hunt, exactly?

The blank face swung toward her. Not your family, it said. Don't worry. That would be . . . rude.

Oh. Well. That—that's good to know, I guess.

Jam almost laughed through her skittering nerves at the thought of this creature being concerned with what Aloe would call home training and what Bitter would call broughtupsy. If the creature showed up in their house, and out of her mother's painting, technically that would make them its hosts. Maybe manners did matter, in that case. Jam looked at the thing, and a whole giggle squeaked out. She knew the sound in her mouth was edged with panic and not a small promise of a full-on freak-out, but come on! Her mother had made that. Her mother, who refused to believe in keeping animals indoors and never let her get so much as a goldfish, had gone and painted a thing with goat legs and ram horns, a thing that could have fallen out of some apocalyptic last pages of an old holy book, a furry, goldfeathered thing that was squatting in the studio like no man's business. The same

Bitter who wouldn't let Jam get a pet had gone and called up a monster.

The thing's head jerked at that, and its fur crackled stiff.

Not a monster, it snapped.

Jam blinked. Um, she thought back. What?

Clearly it could read her thoughts; she was going to have to be careful. The creature put on her mother's voice.

You don't learn nothing from all them lessons about pictures and what you does see with your eyes?

Jam's mouth fell open at the mimicry, and she covered it with a hand. Oh shit.

The creature kept staring at her with no eyes, and Jam pulled herself together. I'm sorry, she replied. That wasn't nice.

She paused. But to be fair, you don't want to tell me what you are, so I'm having to try and guess.

It shrugged and stayed as it was, scary in its stillness.

Jam swallowed hard. The comfort of its awkwardness was gone, and it seemed casually lethal now, like it was lying in wait, like the crouch was a precursor to springing up and that strange, blurry mouth opening and someone's throat being torn out. She was worried about her parents, just a few doors down, despite its reassurances; worried about why it was here and what it was going to do.

She tried to be brave. Well, she said, her hands only a little shaky, at least tell me what I should call you.

The thing looked at her for a long time, drooling smoke. Something about her fear seemed to register with it. As Jam watched, its fur softened and it shifted its stance just a little, draining the menace away.

Well, little girl, it replied, I suppose you can call me Pet.

CHAPTER 3

Jam stared in silence as Pet stood up from its crouch, its full length looming through the air. She was a little less afraid now. Pet reached into its chest and picked out the razor blades that Bitter had embedded in the canvas, dropping them to the floor in tiny clatters. Jam felt her palm twinge in memory, and she curled her fingers around the bandage sticking to her skin.

Why didn't the razors stay inside you?

Pet shrugged. They were not made of paint, it replied. They were not part of the door.

Jam nodded, even though she wasn't quite sure she understood. Pet started walking around and looking through the rest of Bitter's work—piles of drawings stacked on every flat surface, canvases layered and leaning against the walls, shelves full of small sculptures. The moon was still lighting up the studio in a brilliant shine, and it made Pet's feathers and fur glisten. Jam's heart was pounding steadily, driving anxious blood to all parts of her. Maybe, she thought, I'm actually in a dream, like one of those that always feel horribly real but as soon as I wake up, I'll feel silly for even thinking it was real because the real real seems so obvious. Maybe I just need to wake up and that will solve everything.

"You're not dreaming," Pet said, voicing for the first time. The sound was a handful of nails dragging across a mirror. Jam clapped her hands to her ears, wincing, and Pet cleared its throat.

"Sorry," it said, a bag of broken glass clattering against a wood floor this time. "Still calibrating to this body, this world."

"Still sounds horrible," Jam said aloud. Pet angled its head, and she could almost see it thinking, matching, measuring.

"What about now?" it asked, and the sound was a hand dragged across the taut skin of a drum, low and resonant and clear.

Jam nodded. "That's better. Actually kind of nice."

Pet scoffed deep in its throat and flipped through a pile of charcoal sketches. "Nice. Not one of my concerns in this life, to be nice, to sound nice, what is nice."

Jam rolled her eyes. "Not unpleasant?"

"Your world is unpleasant, your truths are unpleasant, the hunt is unpleasant." Pet looked at her with its goldblank

39

face, and thin tendrils drifted out of its mouth. "But unpleasant things must be done for unpleasant purposes out of unpleasant necessity."

Jam stared. "I have no idea what you're talking about."

Pet stopped for a moment and inclined its head at her. "Job description."

"Okay, so none of what you're saying makes any sense whatsoever." She was voicing more than she normally would, but it felt okay. "Why are you here?"

"To hunt, little girl. I already told you."

Jam paced and spun, throwing up her hands. "No, why are you *here*? Why are you in my house? Why did you come out of Bitter's painting? How am I supposed to keep my parents from finding out about you?" Her parents. She'd forgotten about them, but at the thought of explaining how she'd helped pull a giant creature out of a canvas and into their house, Jam flopped down on the floor and pressed her face into her hands. She shouldn't have messed with the painting without her mom's permission; now look what had happened, now this thing was here and hunting, whatever that meant, and Bitter was going to blame her, it was all her fault. "I'm going to be in so much trouble!" she wailed.

Pet was tilting its head again, humming gently. Its face was as solid as a mask, the interlocked feathers unmoving, yet the way it moved its head, those small angles, they communicated a world. In this case it seemed confused. "What do you mean, keep your parents from finding out?"

Jam looked up at it. "What do you mean, what do I mean? Just . . . just look at you!" She gestured to Pet's hugeness, Pet's horns, Pet's creatureness. "They're totally going to freak out!"

"Don't be silly. Your mother painted me." It put down the sketches it had been looking through, and Jam watched its hands, Bitter's dead hands, touching the sketches that had been drawn by Bitter's alive hands, which had painted these dead hands, which were putting down the sketches drawn by the hand that painted them. Her head was hurting. "I should tell her I've arrived," Pet said, and Jam jumped up, a current of alarm galvanizing her.

"Oh no no no no." She waved her arms at it. "We're not doing that. That's a hard no."

Pet cocked its head at her briefly, then started toward the door. Jam ran and blocked it, stretching her arms out past the doorframe. It seemed incongruous in that moment for her to be facing down a seven-foot-tall creature with gold claws and bloody horns, but anyone who had ever seen Bitter lose her temper would probably agree that between Pet and Bitter, Pet was the less scary option. "No! I need you to stay here until I can figure something out, please! If she finds out about this, I'm so dead. I'm not supposed to touch

41

her paintings before they're dry, let alone pull something out of one!"

Pet reached out to lift Jam, with Bitter's obscene dead hands around her ribs, and set her aside firmly. "You will be safe. Don't worry."

Jam groaned. "I don't mean that she's literally going to kill me—"

Pet opened the door and stepped out, bending its neck to clear the doorway. The tip of one horn put a gouge in the paint as Pet walked into the house.

Jam stared after it, her mouth open. "Never mind. She's literally going to kill me." The studio air around her didn't disagree. Pet's footsteps were singing through the floor like mallets striking an ocean of drumskin, and they were heading straight for her parents' bedroom. Jam stayed frozen in place for a few seconds before forcing her legs to move and running after Pet, who was already opening the bedroom door and stepping inside. There was a click as it flicked on the light switch, and then the soft ringing of its voice.

"Apologies for interrupting your sleep," it said.

Jam whirled through the door just in time to see both Aloe and Bitter sit up, sleep slithering away from them, leaving that unpleasant disorientation of an unexpected awakening. Aloe gave out a startled shout, and Bitter's cry was brief and sharp, a stab into the bedroom air. Jam was expecting them to go unhinged, to scream endlessly at the thing standing before them, but there were a few moments of shocked silence instead as Pet stared at them and they stared at Pet. Finally Aloe broke the silence, his eyes narrowed and his voice tight.

"You can't be serious," he said. Jam pressed herself against the dresser, practicing being invisible and waiting for when she, specifically, would be in hot water, as Aloe liked to say. Her father dragged his hand over his face, then massaged his eyes with his fingertips before looking at Pet again. "Mba, it's a lie. This has to be a joke."

Not taking her eyes off Pet for one second, Bitter stretched out a hand and blindly patted their duvet and pillows before finding Aloe's arm and squeezing the flesh of his bicep. "You seeing what I seeing?"

Aloe jerked his arm away and flung the covers off his legs so he could get out of the bed. "Are you actually mad? Of course I'm seeing what you're seeing! Am I blind?" He pressed his hands to his head and paced next to the bed, then turned to Bitter and smacked his palms against the mattress. "You said this nonsense would never happen again, Bitter!"

Shock hooked into Jam like a riptide. Wait, again? Again?!

Bitter was still staring at Pet. She raised her shoulders slowly and let them drop. "I don't know how this happened, Aloe. True talk. This . . . this can't be real."

Jam's father was shouting now. "Don't talk rubbish! Is it not your painting that's standing here in our bedroom? And you're opening your mouth to tell me you don't know how this happened! Are you serious?" He stopped, abruptly quiet, and sagged. "I should have never let you finish painting it," he said, his voice dropping. "I knew this would happen. I could feel how hungry it was to become real."

Bitter just kept staring at Pet, and Aloe slapped his forehead, pitching his voice loud again. "It's as if I learned nothing from last time!"

Jam stared at both her parents, numb and confused. They weren't terrified. How were they not terrified? How were they talking about agains and last times, actually having an argument while Pet stood there patiently, its face as still as metal, almost a statue cast against the pale tangerine of their bedroom wall. Bitter turned her head to glare at her husband, and Jam could almost smell her mother's temper as it began to stir, boiling in her chest under her silk nightgown.

"You know, boy, my ears must be plug up. I could swear you just tell me something about letting me paint? Like you does give me permission to make work?" Her voice was snakesweet and precise.

Aloe glared right back at her. "My friend, vex if you want to vex. Me, all I know is that I am looking at that monster you painted with your own hands. Looking at it with my own two koro-koro eyes as it's standing in front of us, and you want to come and say it's not your fault? Try it!"

Jam's parents were too heated to notice how Pet hissed and crackled when Aloe used the word "monster," but Jam felt and heard it not only in the sound waves that bruised the air but also in the floorboards of the house, a hackled warning that neither Bitter nor Aloe was paying attention to. It was amazing how they had clearly seen but were ignoring Pet. Jam wanted to move, to say something to them, to sign something to them, but she was fixed in that corner, made of stone. Whenever she was really scared or freaking out, the same thing always happened: she began to dissociate, reality loosening around her like a hammock deconstructing itself, spilling her out into sands of nothingness.

Jam pressed her fingers against the dresser, trying to ground herself, trying not to cry, but it was hard, it felt impossible. Her parents were fighting, yelling at each other in front of her, in front of Pet, who had pulled back into its aura of lethal, who was now a snarl embodied, danger that she had brought into the house. All this was her fault, all of it, and she had broken their world, allowed something else into it, allowed not just Pet but conflict between two parents who usually did nothing more than lovingly bicker, and now nothing felt safe and nothing felt okay and it was all her fault. Jam squeezed her eyes shut, the dresser like dreamwood under her hands, all the sound blurring into one raucous whine in her ears. Her fear narrowed and hardened into something numb and old; her pulse loosened. She dropped her hands to her sides and opened her eyes to a world that wasn't real anymore. Her parents were puppets, animated before her, and Pet was turning its head slowly, as if it could smell how quickly she was floating away. Jam watched as it stepped in and pulled her with a feathered arm, placing her body against its streaked fur.

Its hands were chilly, but its torso was warm, unexpectedly so. She hadn't thought it would be; she'd thought it would be cold, like lonely paint or something. There was even a pulse under the fur, a slow and powerful beat that pressed against her flesh. If she hadn't gone numb, then she might have been frightened, but nothing matters when it's not real.

Bitter was defending herself to Aloe now. "I'm telling you, I couldn't have made the painting come alive! You don't remember the last time? It takes blood, Aloe, the work does always take blood before something like that could happen."

"Are you sure, Bitter? Not even by accident? Not even one drop?"

"Not even a drop! I make damn sure of it, ever since then. You think I want to call up a monster?"

This time Pet growled aloud, an angry beastsound that shredded the air in the bedroom. Both Jam's parents snapped their heads around, their faces suddenly taut with fear. Jam felt the vibrations of the growl rattle and rumble through her, leaving a trembling aftertaste. Bitter's hand flew to her mouth when she saw Jam being held by the creature, and Aloe's skin went gray.

"No," he said, "no, not my daughter. Let her go. Let her go!"

"You two are scaring her," Pet said, its voice level. "Are you not ashamed, are you not full of shame, see how shameful you shamelessly shout about me being here, not once thinking if your child was safe, without noticing her, you shame things, where are your eyes, they are not clouded by shame, but maybe they should be."

"We thought she was sleeping," Bitter whispered, her voice thick with frightened tears. "Jam-jam, sweetness, you all right?"

Jam nodded but didn't move. It wasn't that she didn't want to run to her parents now that they were looking at her again, now that she wasn't invisible, or that she wanted to stay next to Pet—it was that neither option seemed to matter very much at the moment. Bitter stepped forward, her gaze flickering between Jam and Pet's motionless face.

"I could take she from you?" she asked, stretching her

arms out to Jam but talking to Pet. The creature hesitated, then nodded and lifted its arm, letting Bitter pull Jam away and back, closer to the bed. Aloe wrapped his arms around both of them and kissed Jam's head over and over. His gray T-shirt was soft against her cheek and smelled like lemons.

"I'm sorry," he whispered. "We didn't know you were in the room. Are you okay?"

Jam nodded, her neck almost automated at this point. Bitter and Aloe exchanged quick looks, reunited in their protectiveness over their daughter.

"What do you want?" Aloe asked Pet, his jaw hard. "Why did you come here?"

Pet's head swiveled thoughtfully. "Here to hunt. Hunt the hunted. Hunt as a hunter."

Bitter kept staring at it, as if she was just admitting to herself that it was really there. She put a hand on Aloe's shoulder, her face slack with shock. "They always come for a reason, remember?" Her voice trembled and faded as she spoke.

Aloe shook his head, shadows swirling in his eyes. "That was a long time ago," he bit out. "We're not doing that again." He glared at Pet, "You can't be here."

Pet dipped its head. "And yet . . ."

"I said no. This is a new Lucille. We're safe. There are no more monsters."

Pet's mouth stretched in amusement, and a sheet of smoke dripped out. "You keep lying that lie, liar."

Aloe stiffened and Jam looked up at him. "It's not a lie. This is Lucille." He said it like it was a prayer he was clutching in both hands.

Pet turned its head slightly, more toward Bitter. "You are the one who made the door."

"I didn't make no key," Bitter countered. "So how you pass through, creature?"

Pet raised a long arm and pointed with Bitter's corpse finger at Jam. "The girl. She bled."

Bitter looked down and took hold of Jam's face, her voice ringed with alarm. "Yuh get blood on the canvas, doux-doux?"

Jam lowered her eyes. "Accident," she whispered, then rubbed her fist to her chest, palm down, an apology.

"Nothing to be sorry for, sweetness. Nothing at all." Bitter hugged her tight, her face old with worry.

"You couldn't have known," Aloe added, and his voice shook only a little.

Bitter looked back at Pet. "So what you here for, then? What is it you want?"

Pet crouched down and slid its spine from side to side, as if stretching. "It is not a what. It is a who. The why is monstrous. The when is here."

Jam drew away from her parents slightly, stepping closer to Pet. Aloe began to reach to pull her back, but Bitter stopped him. "Leave her," she whispered. "It can't hurt her; she the one who brought it over, not the one it looking for."

"Oh, it's now you want to trust it?"

His wife cut her eyes at him. "You know, you does real act as if you weren't there when all this happen first time," she hissed. "I know you does like to forget things when it convenient, but turn on your brain and use your sense. You remember how this work."

Aloe grimaced but didn't argue. He took Bitter's hand instead, and they watched their daughter.

Jam stood in front of Pet. Her stomach was knotting up. If Pet had come to hunt someone, it couldn't be a coincidence that it had come through her and her mother. She switched back to talking to it in her head.

Can you tell me who you came to hunt? she asked.

Pet's head angled down to face her. A monster, it replied, and Jam's stomach plummeted. They looked at each other, a silent understanding thrumming between them. It was an answer she'd been expecting, without knowing she'd been expecting it. Of course there were still monsters, Jam thought. Could you really make something stop existing just by shoving it away somewhere else?

"Jam, what are you doing?" Aloe's voice interrupted, and Jam held up a hand to silence him.

Who's the monster? What does it look like?

Pet hummed, a light vibration shaking through the room. I don't know yet, I am rife with unknowns, part of the hunt is to make the not-known known. Not just to me, or us, but to the not-knowers, so that they may know, the truth is in the knowing.

But how are you going to find it, then?

Pet's voice turned sarcastic again. I feel, little girl, that you're rather missing the point of this being a hunt.

Jam glared at it. Every hunt has to start somewhere, she snapped back. You have to have a place to begin.

Pet reached out with its impostor hand and absentmindedly picked out part of Jam's sleep-flattened afro with its fingers. It was something Bitter would do, almost as if the hands had retained some memory of her mother. I do have a beginning, it admitted.

Jam folded her arms. Okay, then. Tell me.

Pet withdrew its arm and patted down a reddened tuft of fur on its chest.

The house of Redemption, it replied.

CHAPTER 4

After that, Bitter and Aloe sent Jam to bed. She tried to argue with them, but her parents were firm, paying attention now, putting space between her and Pet.

"We could handle it from here, sweetness," Bitter said.

It's not fair! Jam signed. *I want to stay. I'm the one who brought it over!*

"You're a child," Aloe said, his voice a thick line. "It's two o'clock in the morning, and your mother's painting is standing here in our bedroom." He shook his head, irritated. "It's enough. Go and sleep."

Bitter rolled her eyes. "It right there, you don't have to keep calling it a painting."

"I will call that thing whatever I want to call it," Aloe snapped, and Jam shot a worried glance at Pet, expecting it to react to the hostility in her father's voice. But Pet hadn't moved; it just kept watching them with its implacable face, its weight loud loud loud in the floorboards, translating directly to Jam's feet.

Bitter pulled Jam into a hug, kissing her face. "Go to sleep, doux-doux. Come morning and all will be well, I promise you."

Jam didn't believe her, but the silk of Bitter's nightgown was soft against her cheek, and Jam felt a wave of exhaustion drag over her. The spike of the past hour or so began to plummet into a crash, adrenaline abandoning her body. Bitter kept an arm around her and steered Jam toward the door.

"Taking the girl to she room," she said, directing her words at Aloe, pretending that she wasn't talking to Pet, getting its permission to remove Jam. Everyone could feel how the creature was focused on the young girl, the way its edged protectiveness was biting through the air. Bitter was being careful.

Jam twisted around to look at Pet. Will you be here in the morning? she asked, just between the two of them.

It gave her a golden nod. What must be hunted must be hunted, whether it is night or day, no matter how long it takes, it answered. I will be here, little girl.

She nodded and let Bitter take her to her room, let her mother tuck her into bed the way she used to when Jam was smaller. It felt comforting this time, a memory of a ritual that gestured safety.

"Where you put your bonnet?" Bitter asked as Jam climbed into the bed and slid her legs between the cotton sheets. She patted under her pillows, then looked around the room and pointed to a small puddle of satin lying on the floor. Bitter picked it up and stretched the elastic to fit it over Jam's afro. She adjusted it against her forehead and Jam lay back against her pillow, watching her mother watching her. Bitter looked so worried.

"You could sleep, Jam-jam?" she asked.

Don't worry, Jam signed. *I'm good*. It was almost a convincing lie.

Her mother sighed. "I real sorry about the painting. Wasn't supposed to happen."

Jam shrugged and managed a smile. "It's not that scary."

Bitter gave her a sad smile back. "My brave girl," she murmured. For a moment it looked like she wanted to stay with Jam, make sure she really was okay. There was a time when she would sit beside Jam's bed and read her N. K. Jemisin books until Jam drifted off, only leaving when sleep wrapped heavy around the room. But this time Jam could see how Pet's presence was bothering her, how Bitter needed to go and handle that. Jam knew that her mother would want answers, explanations, things unraveled into a pattern that she could accept as rational. Bitter always needed to organize, to tidy up, and right then Pet was an explosion of loose ends she couldn't ignore. Jam decided to forgive her for leaving.

"Goodnight, darling." Bitter switched off the light and shut the door behind her. Ever since she was a child, Jam had hated having the hallway light spilling into her room; she'd always preferred the night to enfold her in its full black. As the song of her mother's footsteps faded through the floorboards, Jam let out a breath that had been choked in her chest and stared up at the ceiling, air spooling out from her mouth into the nothingness around her. Her lungs felt unstable, jittery. She tried to imagine Bitter and Aloe alone with Pet, Pet's bulk filling up their bedroom, Aloe's scared anger bouncing helplessly off it. They would be fine; she knew they would be fine. Pet wasn't going to hurt them. It didn't hurt anything it wasn't hunting, somehow she already knew and trusted and believed that, and besides . . . what it was hunting was in Redemption's house.

A vision of her best friend floated across Jam's mind: his smile, his wrapped hands after fight training. Was he being hurt right now by the monster? Why hadn't he said anything to her? Or maybe nothing had happened yet, maybe Pet was there to stop something from happening. That loosened Jam's anxiety, but not by much. Redemption could take care of himself, she hoped. He'd been a fighter since he was little; he was fast and strong, and who could hurt him? Who would even want to hurt him? He was threaded with nothing but gentleness. Even when he fought, Redemption fought for the beauty of what his body could do, for the frailty of being human, the power and vulnerability tangled up in being flesh. It wasn't personal; it wasn't about his ego. It was about being alive. She remembered when he'd explained this to her, when she'd asked him why he loved something so violent.

"I don't hold violence in my hands," he'd answered, holding them up in front of his face. He and Jam had been lying on a grassy hill behind the school, one they liked to roll down, watching the sky bump and skip in hiccuped blue as gravity played with them. Jam had her head on his shoulder, and Redemption smelled like cut grass and salt and himself. When his voice had started deepening and his shoulders grew broader, his throat ridged, Jam had been fascinated—it was what would have happened to her in another time, another life. She watched as he rotated his wrists to look at his palms and then the backs of his hands, a few nicked scars marking his knuckles.

You fight, she'd said. Of course you hold violence in your hands, she meant.

Redemption heard what she hadn't said out loud, and shook his head. "Here," he said, tapping his chest. "Here is where I hold it, and I look at it and I fold it into something else. Even when I fight, it's not about letting it out. Especially when I fight."

Jam frowned and he took her hand in his, running his fingers over the tendons that traced to her fingers.

"We think we're so strong," he explained. "Some people want to show how strong they are when they fight, they want to prove it by grinding the other person down."

You don't?

He bent her fingers one by one, cracking the knuckles. "For what? We're both alive when we fight. We're magnificent; we're testing our aliveness against each other. How fast is your alive? How smooth is your alive? How hard, how resilient? We're alive because we can be hurt; we're alive because we can heal. I think it's beautiful. It's why I fight."

Jam smiled. *Uncle Hibiscus teach you that?*

Hibiscus was Redemption's trainer, a tall man with muscles like jerky, tough and lean, faster than a snakestrike, and most of all, one of the angels of Lucille. He was a rare example of someone who had been key to the revolution but chose not to get involved in leadership when it was all over. "I just wanted us to get free," he always said. "I was useful for the time." When people asked him if he'd ever get involved again, he would shrug. "Call me when we need to fight," he'd say.

Hibiscus also didn't like talking about the revolution; he wasn't interested in reliving the old days. "We left them behind for a reason," he said. There were rumors about where he'd learned to fight like that, what he'd done during the revolution, why he didn't want to talk about it. When Bitter told Jam that the angels must have had to do dark things, hard things, Jam had thought of Hibiscus and the way his eyes sometimes looked like sad stones embedded in his head. He had no children, just a wife, Glass, who ran a small healing spa next to the gym Hibiscus owned, where he trained Redemption and a couple of other kids.

"Hibiscus is teaching me many things," Redemption answered. "What to bring into the ring, what to leave out of it. It's a good way to think about life." The two of them had remained on the grass until the chill of evening started to set in, then they'd gone home—Jam to her whispering floorboards and Redemption to what Jam now saw as a sweet-laced trap, his home that was a monster harbor.

She turned over in her bed and draped an arm off the edge, her fingers skimming the wood of the floor. It was another way of listening to the house, touching it directly, fine-tuning the vibrations that were coming from her parents' bedroom. They were faint, deliberately so; her parents were probably trying not to wake her up or alarm her. But Jam could still feel the anxiety and fear like a spilled sourness

58

soaked up by the floor, circulating through the house. She could feel Pet's cool weight, indifferent to Bitter's distress and Aloe's anger. It was calm even as her parents' emotions spiked and ebbed, twisted and spat. Pet remained one steady, humming, unmoved line.

Eventually, when Bitter's and Aloe's sounds became tired, pleading even, Pet stirred, but only to fade. Jam could feel that it was gone. No, not gone . . . it had moved. She pressed her fingers harder against the floor. Ah, to the studio. Maybe it was pretending to be a painting again. Jam wanted to stay awake and think about what to do, what they had talked about once she'd left, but she was tired, as if a blanket made of world was pressing down on her. She pulled her hand up and slipped it into the cool under her pillow, sleep diving over her like a wave.

Bitter and Aloe were in the kitchen when Jam came down in the morning, still wearing her pajamas. She'd brushed her teeth and put her hair in four rough braids after dampening it with water, little things to delay coming downstairs and facing the conversation she knew was lurking, waiting. It was rare that Jam felt distinct from her parents—those moments when she was reminded that while in some ways they were a unit of three, in other and older ways, Bitter and

Aloe were a unit of two and she, Jam, was an addendum. A loved and cherished addendum, sure, but still an addendum. This morning felt like such a moment.

Jam knew they'd talked and come to some sort of decision while she was asleep—the house was faintly anxious but firm underneath, mirroring their loud emotions—so Jam had braced herself for whatever they wanted to tell her about Pet. She was hoping they weren't upset with her for what had happened in the night, for cutting herself on the canvas and not telling them, for having a creature shock them out of sleep. She stepped into the kitchen, frowning when she saw her parents. They both looked too brittle; she didn't like it, the way fatigue was ringing their eyes in dark circles. Bitter was refilling her cup with coffee, wearing a tank top and gray shorts, her legs wild lengths extending out. Leafy plants lined the walls, and the skylight bathed the table in the center of the room in morning sun. It was always crowded with succulents that Bitter kept buying at the farmers' market and Jam kept trying to relocate into other parts of the house so they could actually use the table. Aloe was standing at the stove, barefoot and in a rumpled jalabiya, stirring a pan. A chopping board lay on the counter next to him, littered with onion skins, chili ends, and squeezed limes. Jam could smell the saltfish buljol he was making, and as they heard her enter, they both turned and smiled in a way that was designed to hide their worry but failed terribly.

"Good morning, my daughter." Aloe spooned out some buljol on a plate, sprinkled finely chopped shadowbeni as a garnish, and handed it to Jam. There was also sliced avocado drizzled with lime juice and three triangles of toast, already buttered. "If you want more, come and take," he said. Jam signed a quick thank-you and sat down at the table, moving a few tiny, bright cacti out of the way. Bitter joined her, cupping her long fingers around the curve of the coffee mug.

"You sleep okay, doux-doux?"

Jam nodded, arranging buljol and avocado on her toast. She could still feel Pet faintly from the studio.

Aloe sat down as well, leaving his plate empty on the counter. "We want to talk to you about what happened last night," he said.

Bitter glared at him. "Relax yourself. Let the child eat she food first."

I'm okay, Jam said. She just wanted to get it over with.

Her father put a hand on her shoulder. His panic from the previous night was gone, replaced by a worried resolve. Jam knew the expression well; she'd seen it on his face at enough doctor appointments. It was the look he wore when he'd channeled his fear about everything into the singular focus of protecting her, when he had made decisions that could soothe his anxiety with their firmness, their surety.

"We have something to tell you," he said, then glanced at Bitter and back to Jam, before taking a deep breath. "This isn't the first time something like this has happened with your mother's work." He paused, gathering his voice to say more. It seemed difficult. "A long time ago, when we were maybe a little older than you or around your age," he continued, "something came through a painting." Jam watched her father's face drift into a twisted but soft sadness. "It's strange how we can remember so much of it after all this time, how it felt, what happened afterward," he said, his words getting quieter. "I wish still, every day, that we could forget."

Jam bit down on her toast and looked at her mother with wide eyes, unwilling to break the spell of her father's remembering. Their reaction last night had told some of this story plainly enough, but still, hearing it said outright was something else. Bitter caught the curiosity leafing out from Jam's eyes and shook her head.

"The details aren't important," she said. The sadness was in her eyes too, but she was armoring it away, locking it into a box even as she spoke. "Just know many bad things came from that. Plenty people got hurt. I don't want you forced into the kinds of decisions I had to face."

"It was a different time," Aloe interjected quickly. "There

were monsters to hunt; that part was understandable. But Lucille has changed. This one has to have the wrong place."

Bitter nodded. "We think the creature must be mistaken, you see."

"A dangerous mistake."

"It came out into the wrong time, that's all."

"It just needs to go back now," Aloe said. "It's all a misunderstanding."

Jam turned her head from one to the other, waiting for the rest of it. Her parents exchanged looks stuffed with silent words; then Bitter put down her coffee mug and leaned forward.

"You know how the creature came out of the painting, Jam-jam?"

Jam dusted crumbs off one hand and signed a correction: *Pet.*

Bitter paused, her eyebrows knotting. "What?"

Jam almost rolled her eyes, spelling it more slowly. *P. E. T.*

"What do you mean, 'pet'?" Aloe leaned forward as well. "You tried to pet it, or what?"

"That's its name," Jam said, her voice unexpected in the kitchen's air.

Both her parents jerked back in surprise, then looked at each other again. Jam sighed and went back to her food. They had such loud conversations around her even when they weren't using their words, as if she couldn't understand all the other kinds of languages that didn't need sound. This one, the one they were speaking with their eyes, was saying that they were now even more worried than they had been before, now that they knew Pet had a name. So there had to be something about the name that bothered them. Maybe it made Pet seem more like an individual, not just a random creature popping out of a painting. Maybe it had something to do with whenever this had happened before with Bitter's work. Jam had no idea, and she could tell that her parents were busy thinking in a small, separate bubble that was about protecting her but didn't actually include her, the bubble that was their relationship, their marriage, somehow none of her business. She didn't try to interfere. The buljol was salty in her mouth, smeared smooth with avocado, small crunches of onion and toast fragments. Jam focused on that and waited till they decided what they were or were not going to tell her.

"How do you know it has a name?" Aloe asked. "Did you give it one?"

Oh, still on the name, then. Jam shrugged. *It told me.*

"It told you it have a name?" Bitter asked.

Close, but not technically. *Told me what to call it,* Jam answered. What you were called and what your name was were not the same thing, she knew that much.

64

Aloe was frowning, focused on her. "You're not scared of it?" he asked.

Jam shrugged again but didn't say anything past that. It was clear that her parents were scared of Pet in a way that was different from hers. She'd never met anything like it before, never seen a painting burst at its seams in that way, but they had. Maybe that's why they were more afraid: they knew things she didn't know, things they didn't want to share, things that were connected to Pet in patterns Jam couldn't see yet. But there was something off about it. They were treating Pet as if it was dangerous, and it wasn't as if it wasn't—Jam had felt enough of the menace Pet did a good job of concealing to know that, yes, Pet was dangerous. It was just that . . . she knew it wasn't dangerous to her. And that seemed to be where she and her parents were diverging.

Bitter took Jam's hand and turned it over to expose the bandage on her palm. Jam looked up into the black wells of her mother's eyes.

"You cut your hand in the studio, ent?" Bitter asked her gently.

Jam nodded and her mother patted her hand, releasing it. Aloe was visibly distraught, but he pressed his mouth closed.

"It's how it does happen," Bitter murmured. "Blood calling."

What does it mean? Jam asked.

"It's what brings them over," Aloe said. His voice was wound so tight, Jam was surprised it wasn't shaking. "We never figured out the exact details of how; that first time was enough."

But you knew it was blood, Jam said. She watched their eyes slide again into an unfocused memory, the slight wince that shuddered under Bitter's skin. Whatever they kept remembering, it was painful.

"We knew," her mother said, with a full stop that barricaded any further questions. "But hear me now. You could reverse this. Send it back."

"It has to listen to you," Aloe added.

Understanding clicked into place in Jam's mind. *Because of the blood,* she said.

They looked back at her sadly. "We don't like to ask you to do this," Bitter said. "But once you send it back, everything good, just so, everything nice."

Aloe put his hand on Jam's shoulder again. "All you have to do is tell it, and it has to obey you. It will be all over. Kpọm." He snapped his fingers, a small bullet of sound breaking against his palm.

She could feel how badly he wanted that to be true, how badly they both wanted it. They didn't know the bit about Redemption, but Jam already felt as if it wouldn't matter. At some point last night, they'd decided that Pet was wrong and that Jam would be safer without it there. They wouldn't believe Pet, not even for Redemption. Adults were like that so much of the time, inflexible when they thought they had something to protect.

What if you're both wrong? she said, her hands flurrying. *It said the monster was in Redemption's house. What if something bad is happening there?* She was surprised at herself for telling them that, but she had to try. If Redemption's safety was at stake, then it was worth it, this desperate attempt to get them to open their eyes and change their minds.

Jam knew she'd lost when Bitter just smiled back and touched her face like a brief feather. "It knows Redemption means a lot to you," her mother said. "I'm not surprised it could say something like that, to persuade you to let it stay."

"We've done this before," Aloe said. "You have to trust us, my dear."

Jam lowered her head under the weight of their blinkered love and pushed her plate away, half her food untouched and the rest of it sour in her stomach. *Okay,* she signed, and got up from her chair. Bitter stood as well, wringing her hands together. They all knew Jam was going back to the studio, where Pet was waiting, either in the air of the room itself or in the air beyond it, on the other side.

"I could come too," her mother offered, but Jam shook her head, refusing. She could feel their heavy gazes drag across her back as she left the kitchen, and she knew that they'd feel better if she said something, anything, that showed that she understood their decision and had chosen to be on their side, a unit of three again. But Jam was silent as she walked out, because the only thing in her chest was a low kind of bitterness, a sort of feeling trapped and not being heard. They hadn't cared when she mentioned Redemption, and she'd anticipated that, but it was still a disappointment, to be waved aside so easily. Bitter and Aloe had decided as a unit of two—they could sit with their decision then, just the two of them alone. Jam went up to the studio, feeling close to bursting into tears. She couldn't tell if it was from fear or sadness or anger or frustration; it was just there, right behind her eyes.

The studio door was firmly closed, and Jam took a deep breath before turning the knob. It opened silently, and as she stepped in, she felt Pet's presence accumulate, the loudness of it growling through the floorboards and into the soles of her feet. Jam closed the door behind her and looked around.

Pet stepped out from a corner, still massive, still gold and streaked fur and hardblood curled horns.

"Here to banish me, little girl?"

Of course it already knew. Jam shrugged and stared at the patterns on its face.

"Here to erase me," it continued, its voice trailing looped faint smoke into the air. "Here to push me into the black, away from the eyes, I am too loud, too saying loud things, too looking loud. Your parents think if you wipe me away, you can wipe away the inside of my mouth, the things I came with that live there. They don't even know, they know enough to want me gone, they know the shape of the thing from the edges. What do you think, little girl?"

Jam gazed at the floor, focusing on a small splatter of blue paint that looked as if the sky had bled and no one had cleaned it up in time. "I think they're afraid," she said.

Pet leaned its head back and forth, horns tipping over, goldfeathered throat exposed and then curved forward.

"Hmmm," it said. "What else do you think? You want to say the line, the striking line, the erasing line?" It sat down carefully in front of her, avoiding its own torn canvas in the middle of the floor, folding its great muscular legs and draping its arms in loose lines. Its hands dangled, the metal talons dragging mild grooves as Pet moved to get comfortable on the floor. "What do you want, what will you do, who are you?"

The studio floor was a distressed brown around the stain of sky. Jam balled her hands up into fists, squeezing tightly. She'd never hidden things from her parents before, not really. It was hard to keep secrets; you had to keep track of them, regulate how they moved through your body, make sure they didn't swerve and jump out of your mouth. She'd never really disobeyed them before either, not like this, not in a way that mattered like this. It made her feel separate and lonely. Pet kept looking at her with no eyes.

Jam closed hers and rallied her thoughts, trying to stay focused. She was not alone; Pet was here. If she split from her parents, it wouldn't really be two of them and one of her; it would be two and two, if she didn't send Pet away. But more importantly, Pet was here for a reason.

There was a monster in Redemption's house.

Even if Pet was wrong, like Bitter and Aloe thought, that wasn't a risk she could take. It was too big. It was her best friend; it was Redemption. And if Pet was right, and there was a monster there, then it meant no one knew about it, no one had caught whoever it was, and Redemption was still in danger.

Boiled down to that, it was a simple choice. Her parents floated away. Jam opened her eyes, and colored spots hovered in the air before her.

"I need you to stay," she said.

CHAPTER 5

Late the next morning, Jam was twisting her hair in her bedroom, smearing whipped shea butter on her palms and apply-
ing it in sections while soca music played over her speakers.
Pet was standing in a corner of the room, its head moving in
small jerks as it followed her arms, watching her. They were
talking without sound; Jam didn't want her parents to know
Pet was still around, that she had disobeyed them, and since
Bitter and Aloe couldn't feel things through the house the
way that Jam could, she could hide Pet in a mute cocoon.

What happens now? she asked. How does this work?

Pet slowed the movements of its head to focus on her.
The first step to seeing is seeing that there are things you do
not see, it said.

Jam paused and frowned. I don't understand.

The creature sighed and rustled its fur a little. If you
do not know there are things you do not see, it said, then
you will not see them because you do not expect them to be

there. You think you see everything, so you think everything you see is all there is to be seen.

So, there are things hiding? Jam said. And you can't find them unless you're looking . . . like there's the stuff I can see but there's more?

Pet tilted its head in approval. Yes, it replied, there is more. There is the unseen, waiting to be seen, existing only in the spaces we admit we do not see yet.

Jam went back to her hair, dabbing castor oil on her ends as she worked through a few tiny knots. So you'll go looking for the unseen things, since you're the hunter and all that.

Pet fell silent, and a vague unease began rolling off it.

Jam turned, wiping her hands on her jeans. I said, you'll go looking, right? That's your job, that's the whole point of you being here. I bring you over, and you take care of Redemption.

Pet grunted. Not exactly, little girl.

What do you mean, not exactly?

A hunter, yes, Pet explained, but a hunter alone? No. The child they call Redemption is important to you, and you are important to the hunt for the monster in the house of Redemption.

Jam backed up. I don't want to hunt anyone, she said. That's supposed to be your job!

Pet shrugged, its metal shoulders glinting as the feathers

slid over each other. I am not allowed to move so freely in this your world, it said with a trace of bitterness that pooled, oily, in the air between them. That is why you are important: there must be a hunter like me; there must be a hunter who is human, who can go where I cannot go, see what I cannot see.

Then what do *you* do? Jam snapped, her words heavy with contempt laid over a skeleton of fear. She didn't want to call Pet useless, not directly, but the word was hidden under her words, and Pet picked it up.

The creature growled low in its throat and changed its body language, small shifts that bled naked menace into the room. Jam flinched—she had become used to the toned-down version Pet had been showing her, a version that allowed her to forget, even while looking straight at it, what exactly it was. A terror that had climbed through the night and into her life.

I will, Pet snarled, do what you cannot do.

Jam looked away; it was impossible not to. Her hands shook a little as she turned back to her mirror, trying to play it cool and not glance at Pet's reflection. She didn't want to show it she was scared. The soca music played on as she worked on another section of her hair, hectic steel pan and percussion thumping through the air, her spine prickling. Pet heaved a sigh and pulled itself together, sheathing the threat it had been sending out. The air settled into a hesitant peace.

I know it is difficult, little girl, it said. Our concerns are aligned in this: you want the safety of the child they call Redemption, and I want the monster who threatens that. A hunt can take a long time. A hunter must be patient. For now, we do not know enough. Your job is to find out more, and all you have to do is be willing to see, to admit that there are unseens waiting to be seen. Do you understand?

Jam nodded, even though the fear was still a tangled necklace in her stomach, heavy and iron. Pet came up to her in a single step, its weight silent, like it was both there and not there. It put her mother's severed hand on her shoulder, and its claws curved over her collarbone.

I am sorry I made you afraid. I never mean you any harm. I am here to protect you and the ones you love.

Jam looked at its face in the mirror and nodded. It wasn't really Pet she was afraid of but the job that lay ahead of them, the responsibility, the way she would have to hide it from her parents.

It's going to be fine, Pet said. All you have to do is look. If there is something to see, you will see it.

But where do I look? Jam asked. I don't even know what I'm looking for.

Pet's voice rolled through her head, deep and resonant:

It is simple. Start with your friend. Look for something you have not seen.

They were interrupted by Bitter's voice, carrying down the hall and through the bedroom door, piercing into their small, secret world. "You still want a ride, Jam? I heading out now."

"Where's she going?" Aloe's voice was faint from the living room.

"You know she and that boy go see a movie every weekend." Bitter raised her voice to call out again. "Jam!"

Jam closed her eyes and groaned. She hated having to yell, but she didn't want her mother coming to her room either. "Coming!" she called back, then opened her eyes to look at Pet, half-formed questions lumpy under her tongue.

The creature had already disappeared, leaving her in the empty room with greasy fingertips. She finished her last twist in a hurry, then grabbed her phone and rushed out to meet Bitter.

Her mother touched her face gently. "You doing okay, doux-doux?"

Jam nodded, but Bitter kept looking at her.

"You vex with us for making you send the creature away? It's a lot to deal with, what happened. You want to talk about it?"

Jam shook her head, not meeting her mother's eyes, even

as she felt Bitter's worry sing against her skin. She hadn't quite forgiven either of her parents for being so dismissive of Pet's warning, for not being with her in this hunt. Maybe she wouldn't forgive them until Redemption was safe, and maybe not even then. The drive to the movie theater was quiet, with only the wind breaking against the edge of the windows.

When they pulled up, Redemption was standing on the sidewalk, waiting, tall and whipcord lean. Relief burst large and bright through Jam when she saw him. He was okay. Even if Pet was right and something horrible lived in his house, right now Redemption was there, and he was okay. Jam let her mother kiss her cheek, and then she hopped out of the car and into her best friend's arms. His hugs were her favorite, solid and strong and never halfway. She locked her arm in his as they went into the theater, feeling the flesh of his bicep. He's safe, she told herself. Right now, he's with me and he's safe. If she said it over and over, she wondered if the words would become a spell that would hold true even after he went home.

Jam exhaled when they sat in their seats, welcoming the dark of the large room, the artificial light of the screen that stretched from floor to ceiling, curving in on them. It was a beautiful secret and public place. Redemption reclined his seat and glanced over at her. *You okay?* he signed.

I'm fine. She smiled back, but she knew it didn't look convincing. They'd been friends too long.

Redemption raised an eyebrow and reached over to squeeze her hand. "Whenever you're ready to share, I'm here," he whispered. The light played blue off his dark skin, and Jam patted his cheek, stroking a thumb over the razor of his cheekbone.

Thank you.

She had no idea how she could even start sharing everything that had happened at her house, how she would explain Pet or the warning it had dragged over. How was she supposed to explain that a creature was coming to hunt at his house? Or that Pet's arrival had tossed her out of the world she used to live in and left her floating in an uncomfortable nowhere. Everything looked the same, but nothing was. Being at the movies was an escape into a large cocoon of a story, a step away from the outside. The sound drowned out everything else, the walls were insulation for the next few hours, there was no need to talk or think. Jam could pretend that everything had stopped, and in the space of that pause, she could breathe.

Jam rubbed her upper arm as they stepped outside after the movie; the theater had been chilly, and sometimes the hormone implant in her arm ached when she got cold. Redemption yawned and stretched. "Wanna come over?" he asked.

Sure, she said. They exchanged a quick smile and set off down the sidewalk, Redemption whistling, his arms loose by his sides. Jam put her hands in her pockets, grounding herself in the soft cotton. It was weird to be going over to his house now that she knew what she knew, like she was a spy, almost. Gathering intel for Pet. She didn't like keeping a secret from Redemption, but it wasn't time to tell him about Pet, not yet. Not that telling would even work—you had to see Pet to accept that it was real in this world; the telling would never be enough. Words are never enough for a lot of things. Besides, Jam wanted to be sure that there actually was someone dangerous in his house—not like Pet-dangerous, which felt like a righteous-sword-of-fire kind of danger, but old-school dangerous, monster dangerous.

It had taken the angels a long time to get rid of that kind of dangerous in Lucille; it was a fight that had started decades before even Bitter was born. The revolution had been slow and ponderous, but it had weight, and that weight built up a momentum, and when that momentum finally broke forth, it was with a great and accumulated force. This force washed out the monsters who worked in public spaces, allegedly for the public, but it carried farther, into the homes and schools. It touched everyone; it made change. People started by believing the victims, and once this was apparent that it was safe to report monsters now, more and more people did so. The monsters always tried to apologize when they were caught, using the same slippery words that had worked for them before. They thought it would be enough, that some time would pass and they would be welcomed back as if nothing had happened. They were wrong. There was no twisting away from the repercussions that the angels brought, justice rising like a sun over the hill in a loud morning.

There had been so much counseling, so many treatment programs, so much rehabilitation to be done. So many amends to be made, the makings of how different justice could look. It was no small thing to try to restructure a society, to find the pus boiling away under the scabs, to peel back the hardened flesh to let it out. Jam had heard stories of how horrifying it had been to see the truth of how many monsters there were in Lucille—the public ones, the private ones, the chameleons, the freestyle solitary ones, the charismatic smiling ones. There were so many challenges, like how finding them was one thing but keeping more from forming was another. Like how the work of addressing the wounds they had caused never seemed to end. Bitter had told Jam a little about it, but only a little. The stories seemed to scald her mouth.

"You can't know how happy your father and I were," she'd said to Jam, "to bring you into a life where you eh have to go through things like that."

Jam had thought herself lucky then, and maybe she was still lucky now, but lucky meant very little when there was a chance that a monster had slipped through the cracks, or that one had formed despite all the dismantling the angels had done. They'd done their best to tear apart entire structures, things that made monsters. "We must kill the structures all the way to their roots," the angels had said, "and only then will Lucille be safe."

But something must have been missed, something must have gone wrong, because now Pet was here, an exterminator hunting down the rogue monster plant that had grown in Lucille's reformed garden, a stray and secret kind of dangerous. The seed and stems of it were winding through the walls of Redemption's house, and Jam had no idea how she was now supposed to tell which bits were okay and which bits were monster, if they looked the same as they'd always looked her whole life.

By the time they got to Redemption's house, Jam had pulled up every ounce of courage she could find. This was a mission, and all she had to do was what Pet had suggested: try to see more than she'd been seeing before. Look harder for things she maybe wouldn't have thought existed. It would be like having new lenses put into her eyes, shifting the filter through which she took in everything around her, but Jam was ready. This was her part to play in helping her friend, and she was determined to do it well.

Redemption opened the front door, and Jam followed him into the house. They were almost knocked down by his little brother, who was running full tilt across the foyer while holding a skateboard, his coiled hair squished by a helmet.

"Whoa, whoa, whoa!" Redemption grabbed his brother's shoulders. "Why you running in the house, Moss? You know Mama doesn't like that."

Moss tilted his head up and smiled, a tooth missing. "Mama busy in the kitchen, Mama not noticing nothing! Whisper said I can show my new tricks after dinner, I going to practice now." He twisted out of his brother's hands and waved at Jam. "Hi, Jammy. Bye, Jammy."

Redemption sighed as he watched him hurtle out of sight around a corner. "Boy can't slow down," he said, shaking his head.

Maybe when he breaks his arm again, he'll learn? Jam said.

"Ha! If the first time didn't teach him, another one won't."

They took off their shoes and shoved them into the already overflowing shoe rack. Music and voices poured out of the kitchen, pulling them in. Jam could already feel the familiar warmth of Redemption's house wrapping around her like a soft, fuzzy blanket she'd known for years. She let out a breath, and tension she hadn't realized she was still holding unfurled, an open petal in her shoulders. She'd been worried that the house would feel different with what Pet had said, that maybe there'd be a malevolent thread spiking through the air and it would needle its way into Jam's head and she wouldn't be able to hold herself together long enough to find out where it was coming from. But everything felt the same, and same was good; she hadn't been having much same in the last day.

The kitchen in Redemption's house was yellow and enormous, with a long farm table on one end and a large stove system along another wall, green-tiled counters stretching everywhere. An herb basket garden hung from the high wooden beams, and the room was full of Redemption's family, loud and soft and laughing. His mother, Malachite, was punching down bread dough in a large ceramic bowl, the sleeves of her linen shirt rolled up to her elbows, her mouth open in a laugh and her eyes crinkled. His father, Beloved, was sitting on a stool across from her, sketching her face while the recipient of her smile, Redemption's third parent, Whisper, juggled three oranges and a grapefruit, their eyes focused on the fruit, tongue sticking out in concentration. Two of Redemption's uncles were sitting at the long table, picking out stones from trays of dried beans, while his baby cousins played under the table. His aunts would likely be out in the garden, whispering some kind of magic to the plants or pulling up weeds. The uncles smiled and nodded as Redemption and Jam greeted them, then fell back to their tasks, a low hum of conversation flowing across the wood of the table.

Jam watched as Whisper caught the fruits one by one, dropping their torso into a deep and dramatic bow when the performance was complete and the air was empty. Malachite clapped her floury hands together. "You're getting so much better, love!" she said.

"Still only four pieces, though? Up your game, Whis." Redemption grinned as he teased his parent, and Whis grabbed him in a gentle headlock before letting him go.

"You're a rude little rat, that's what you are. Hello, Jam darling. Love those twists."

Thanks, Jam signed, smiling as she gave Malachite a quick hug, breathing in the smell of yeast and flour. The only thing that could smell better would be when the baking was done and there was fresh bread to tear into. Malachite wiped her hands on her batik apron and hugged Jam back, dropping a kiss on her forehead.

"How was the movie?" she asked.

Jam gave her a thumbs-up and then reached across the kitchen island to dap Beloved, who'd reached his fist out from behind his sketchpad, his glasses slipping down his nose.

"You staying for dinner?" Whisper asked. Jam glanced at Redemption, who was pouring out orange juice from the fridge.

"Yeah, of course," he said. "Stay, Jam." He handed her a full glass with pulp floating at the top, and she smiled as she took it.

Okay.

"Perfect," said Malachite. "We're having spatchcocked chicken."

Jam raised her eyebrows. *Fancy.*

"Oh yeah," Whisper replied. "Malachite's roasting them in duck fat."

Beloved closed his sketchpad and gestured to Jam as if he had a secret. "I've got potatoes and root vegetables in the oven," he said in a low voice, "for those principled ones among us who don't particularly feel like eating dead meat."

The other two groaned in unison. "As opposed to alive meat?" Malachite retorted, and even the uncles all the way over at the table laughed. Beloved gave the world a long-suffering look, and Jam leaned against a cabinet with a grin plastered on her face, watching them banter. Even as they teased each other, Redemption's parents were always tracking him with eyes full of love.

The screen door at the back of the kitchen banged open,

and Malachite's sister, Glass, came in, balancing a large box in her arms. She was wearing a white slip dress, and her feet were bare.

"You come in through the garden?" Malachite asked.

"Yeah, girl, parked out back. Your tomatoes looking real good." Glass leaned her head away from the box to greet the rest of the room. "Hey, y'all!"

A chorus of greetings echoed back at her. Beloved hopped off his stool to help her with the box, and Jam gave a shy wave from across the kitchen as Redemption hugged his aunt. "Where Hibiscus at?" Glass asked, looking around for her husband.

Redemption frowned. "I haven't seen him, actually."

"Oh, he's out on the side, trimming back some of those trees for me," Malachite said.

Glass put one hand on her hip and stroked Redemption's cheek with the other. "Y'all ain have training today?"

The boy grinned and did some quick shadowboxing. "Did it in the morning. He made me run like six miles before breakfast!"

"Ooh, chile. He making you work."

"Yeah, your aunt knows the feeling well," Whisper said with a laugh.

Beloved choked on the lemonade he'd just poured for himself, and Malachite threw a tea towel at Whisper, who dodged it, still cackling. "Don't be making jokes like that in front of the children!" she scolded.

Glass went to the fridge, smacking Whisper upside their head on her way. "You nasty," she said.

"You ain never lie."

"That's enough from the both of you." Malachite glared at them before softening her face for Redemption. "Go call your uncle and your brother in, baby." Redemption nodded and dipped out the back door while Beloved snuck a peek under the lid of the box.

"Oh, snap, you made pies, Glass?"

She laughed, tossing blond dreadlocks over her shoulder as she poured herself a drink. "Lord, no, chile. I bought pies." Glass took off the heavy rings she was wearing and slid them into her pocket. "Need some help, Malachite?"

"Shoot, always. Grease those pans for me? These ones just like to watch me work."

"Girl, stop lying." Beloved cut his eyes at her as he put the pies away in the fridge. "You don't let anyone but your sister help in your kitchen."

"Ain't that the truth," Glass agreed, with a little chuckle. She swiped her fingers over an unwrapped slab of butter and began greasing the loaf pans Malachite was going to bake in. Jam put her empty glass down on the counter and exhaled.

Maybe her parents were right.

Maybe Pet had come to the wrong time line, gotten the wrong house. Her eyes moved from face to face in the kitchen, measuring the happiness that permeated their skin, their teeth, their air. Redemption and Hibiscus came in through the back door, the screen swinging, their arms wrapped around each other. Moss thundered underfoot, and Whisper caught him, scolding him about a fresh scrape on his arm. The uncles were picking up babies, and Hibiscus was dropping a kiss on his wife's shoulder. *Hey, Jam,* he said when he saw her. *How you been?*

Hibiscus had learned sign language along with Redemption way back when Jam was little, so they could both talk to her, and it always made her feel warm and lovely that he'd bothered, that he loved Redemption so much it spilled over to Jam. It made him feel like family.

I'm good, she replied. *Chilling.* Hibiscus smiled at her, then leaned over to join Whisper in looking at the scrape Moss had on his arm.

"We've got to clean this out," Whisper was saying. Moss made a high-pitched whine and twisted away from them, darting out of the kitchen. "We're still gonna have to clean it!" Whisper yelled after him.

Hibiscus shook his head. "These kids, man. Stubborn as hell."

"Tell me about it." Whisper passed him a beer, and Jam

let their conversation bleed into the rest of the kitchen as she looked around. She couldn't see how any of this was anything other than safe. This was the kind of home that she sometimes wished she lived in, so full of people that you could never imagine being alone, feeling alone, again. Not that she felt alone with Bitter and Aloe—it was just quieter in their house, with the three of them when they had been three, before she chose Pet and separated herself. There was more space in her house, and with more space you had more places where you could be by yourself. Here it felt like people would be pressing on you wherever you went. To be honest, Jam knew that at any other time, the idea of living in such loving tumult would've made Jam want to crawl out of her skin and leave her body behind for a little private silence somewhere else, but right then she was a little scared and feeling more alone than usual. The thought of being surrounded by people, with all their worlds crowding out hers, of being swaddled with their noise—it felt like maybe it could be a comforting thing.

Her mission crept back into her head: her job was to figure out where a monster could be in all of this. Was it one of these people, each and every one of whom she could swear loved Redemption more than their own life? Where were these unseens she was supposed to see? What was she meant to be looking for?

Jam had grown up with these people. Malachite had made a birthday cake for her each year and even taught her how to pipe bright, glossy icing to spell out her name in a sugary cursive. Whisper had taught her how to braid her hair into two thick cornrows, because neither Bitter nor Aloe had any idea how to. Beloved had sat down with her and Redemption during their first big fight, when they were thirteen, to arbitrate. He'd taught them how to disagree, reminded them how important it was to do so while still showing care and respect for the person you loved. It didn't make sense, what Pet had come across worlds and through a broken canvas to say.

Jam had been there when Hibiscus cried after Redemption won his first fight, in the victory moment when Redemption had kissed his wrapped fist and extended it to his coach from the center of the ring, blood running down the side of his face, his eyes calm and steady. The cameras had caught Hibiscus covering his mouth with one hand, shocked by his own emotion, by the proud tears blurring under his eyelashes. Jam had run up from her seat to the edge of the ring to take Hibiscus's other hand. He'd been surprised by that too; he'd glanced down at her and then back at Redemption, but he squeezed her hand tightly and didn't let go for a while, forgetting even how strong he was. Jam's hand had been numb for ages afterward, but she hadn't minded.

After Jam's surgery, Glass had come by the house every couple of days, massaging her feet and hands, dabbing oils on her temples and scalp, loving her with her hands. These people were family, had *been* family. And now Pet was telling her that one of them was a monster? Standing in the glow of that kitchen, Jam couldn't see it, couldn't believe it. Pet had to be wrong, she decided. Yeah, there was no other option. She would tell it so when she got home. She'd do what her parents had suggested, send it back, fall back into them to become a three again. Redemption was safe, of course Redemption was safe. She was right here; she could see it, feel it. How could some creature from a painting know these people, her people, better than she did?

The decision was a certain and immediate relief. Jam dropped her fear like a winter coat and walked forward to help Whisper set the table as if she was stepping into sunshine, leaving a heaviness pooled on the floor behind her.

CHAPTER 6

It was dark when Jam started walking home, but she hopped through the large patches of yellow streetlight on the side-walk, her steps soft and hopeful. She was going to go home and talk to Pet, explain that she'd been to Redemption's house and seen everything there was to see, explain that everything was fine and Pet could go home, wherever home was for it, a strange world on the other side of a torn canvas. Afterward the picture of her life would click back into positions she knew and recognized, smooth and pretty, with no terrifying ripples.

Jam slid her hands into her pockets and listened to the crickets hidden in the grass, her earphones floating unused around her neck. The fireflies were dancing dots of light in the dark patches, and the air was sweet.

A voice interrupted her thoughts.

You're wrong, you know.

Startled, Jam whipped her head around. Pet was walking next to her, smoke rising off it like indifferent steam. Its arms hung along its sides, and it moved soundlessly, relaxed, as if it wasn't strolling out in the open in the middle of Lucille. Jam glanced at the houses that lined the street, but Pet chuckled, the sound only in both their heads.

Don't worry, little girl. I am an unseen. They can only see you, the one they know to see. It tilted its head and made a small humming sound. Although perhaps you will become a little unseen, since you see unseen things now, especially after you see more of them.

Jam's shoulders relaxed, and she ignored the second part of what it had said. So you're basically invisible?

Pet shrugged. She wondered if it had picked that up from its short time here. You can see me, it said. I am unseen and visible.

Jam nodded and tried not to look too much like she was staring up into the empty air beside her. They walked for a few minutes before she remembered its first words. Wait, she said. What did you mean, I'm wrong?

The creature rolled its head around on its neck. You are not right, it answered. You think you are right, but you are missing things and you are wrong.

Jam folded her arms across her chest, feeling prickly. It

was talking about Redemption's house. You don't know them the way I do, she said.

Pet swiveled its empty face, and a streetlight shone harshly off its metal feathers before sliding away.

That's precisely the point, little girl. Your knowing, you think it gives you clarity, sight that pierces. It can be a cloud, a thing that obscures.

Jam frowned, and Pet rolled its neck again, ruffling its fur. Some of the things you know are not true, it said. You have to learn that things might not be real, even if they look familiar.

You think I'm not seeing something in Redemption's house.

Pet stopped walking. I am not a mistake, little girl.

Jam stopped as well and dropped her head, embarrassed. She wanted to deny that she'd been thinking exactly that, but she couldn't.

Pet's voice was gentle anyway. It's hard to look at things differently, I know.

Jam started walking again, trying not to look too upset. Pet kept up with her easily, its strides swallowing up her smaller steps.

It would be easier if nothing had changed, it continued. If everything was still pretty and safe, yes? Like this little town your angels have made. A pool of water with the moon reflecting in it . . . who would want to throw a stone and break the picture? It is fine to be afraid, to have a fine fear, to not want to cross a fine line.

Jam flinched and curled her hands into fists, burying them deeper in her pockets. I'm not afraid, she hissed.

She didn't want to be called that. Afraid meant being closed and not brave, hiding and not looking.

I looked, she said. I just didn't find anything! That's different.

She tucked her elbows against her, pressing her arms against her ribs, making herself a tight line.

Did you find nothing because there was nothing or because you didn't want to find anything? Pet asked, its quiet bulk moving beside her. It didn't fit on the pavement, so it walked on the road instead, passing through parked cars as if it was spun out of nothing but nightmare and imagination.

Don't tell me what I wanted, Jam snapped.

Is there a want in you I do not see? Pet replied. A want to find a monster, to think something bad could be happening to your friend?

I don't *want* anything bad to be happening to Redemption, Jam said, pushing away tears before they could fall. I don't think there's anything so terrible about that.

Pet stepped in front of her, dropping a knee to the pavement. It became roughly her height, other than the dark red horns rising in the shine of the streetlight, and smoke wafted out of its mouth, smelling like ash.

Listen to me, little girl, it said. You want many things, you are full of want, carved out of it, made from it, yes. But the truth does not care about what you want; the truth is what it is. It is not moved by want, it is not a blade of grass to be bent by the wind of your hopes and desires.

Pet put its hands on her shoulders, leaning its layered face close to hers.

The truth does not change whether it is seen or unseen, it whispered in her mind. A thing that is happening happens whether you look at it or not. And yes, maybe it is easier not to look. Maybe it is easier to say because you do not see it, it is not happening. Maybe you can pull the stone out of the pool and put the moon back together.

Jam was crying quietly now. She could feel both the path Pet's words were taking and the way her fear was trying to cover it up with thick briars of denial. She wanted it to stop, all of it, but Pet kept talking, its voice like many hands dragging over an infinite drumskin, creating a thrum that crept under her skin.

What if you didn't think about what you wanted, what you hoped? Pet asked. What if you thought about what was happening instead? How does that change your wants?

Jam pressed her hands to her face and tried to calm the

trembling inside her. Pet's bulk was casting a black shadow over her, but it felt almost safe, like a shield. She tried to follow its instructions, think about what was actually happening, but she hit a snag almost immediately.

I don't have any proof, she said, dropping her hands. You're the only one saying anything's happening.

Pet's face gleamed in front of her. I am the only one saying so, it agreed. But I came across realms to do my job. You can choose to believe me or not to believe me. The truth does not care. The thing that is happening will happen whether you believe me or not.

Jam stared into its smoke-filled mouth and thought again, this time with the memories of Redemption's laughter-filled house fresh in her mind. If she was wrong, if her sight was wrong and she acted on it and sent Pet away, then she would be turning her back on whatever hurt could be happening there, whatever help she could give.

Pet moved its head, and the smoke angled newly. Do you want to take that risk? it asked, its voice soft inside her skull.

Jam bit her lip. Pet was right, but even if it was wrong, she couldn't take the chance. She wasn't sure how to hold the picture of Redemption's house and the family inside along with the things Pet was saying. It felt like one should push out the other entirely, like both couldn't be real together. Jam wasn't sure what to do about it, but it was clear she couldn't afford to throw the possibilities away without even trying.

It's not that I believe you, she said, after a long pause. I still don't see what could be wrong in that house . . . but I also don't not believe you.

Jam took a deep breath.

If there's something else happening, which I'm not sure there is, then I want to find out, she said. Okay?

Pet released her shoulders and stood up, moving back to her side as they began the walk home again. Okay, it said.

After she got home and Pet faded away, Jam pulled out her tablet and laid it flat on her bed, tapping on the screen to wake it up.

"Call Redemption," she said, her voice low.

The tablet beeped once, then the line started ringing. Jam folded her legs on her egg-blue duvet and waited for Redemption to pick up. It took a few rings before the video call connected and Redemption's face appeared on her screen. His hair and skin were damp, and he was drying himself with a towel.

"Sorry, I was just getting out of the shower," he said, his face stretching into an easy smile. "How you feeling?"

I'm good, she signed, leaning the tablet up on its kick-stand. *You?*

"Chilling." He pulled on a T-shirt and sat down, angling his screen to see her better. "Thanks for coming over today. I know it was a lot of people, I was worried you'd be flooded."

Jam shrugged. *I wanted to show you something,* she said.

His eyes lit up. "Oh, dope."

Jam slid her legs off the bed, taking the tablet with her over to her desk. The heavy library books were there, lying open to the pages with the terrible pictures. They'd been there since the night she brought them home. After Pet arrived, Jam had flipped through the pages, wondering if there was anything in there that looked like it. There hadn't been, which made sense, since Bitter had spun Pet out of nothing, after all.

Jam flipped the camera to show Redemption the illustrations.

"Whoa," he said. "These are wild. Can you zoom in a little?"

She held the tablet closer, scanning it over the pages, mouth-filled wings occupying the screen.

"Those are angels??"

Jam reversed the camera back to her face and nodded, setting the tablet down on her desk.

"Yo, but they look like straight-up monsters, though."

That's what I said, she answered, plopping into a chair. *Bitter said monsters don't look like anything.*

"Monsters gotta look like something," he said. "How else would we know what they were?"

They're all gone. Jam didn't quite believe the line, but they'd been taught it all their lives.

"Okay, fine," Redemption continued, "but monsters must've looked like something at some point. The angels had to identify them, right?"

Some things must have been obvious.

"Well, yeah. Like if someone was hurting other people all the time."

Maybe it's not how people look, it's what they do?

Redemption nodded. "Makes sense."

An easy silence fell, and Jam wondered what to do next. Could she ask him if someone was hurting him, doing things that didn't feel right? How was she supposed to look for the unseen things Pet kept talking about? It wasn't her house, it wasn't as if she could listen to the floorboards talk and trace the secrets. If she could, she'd find the feelings that lay behind the voices when the grown-ups were talking, hunt without moving, just with her hand pressed to the floor.

"I wonder what their criteria were," Redemption said.

Whose? Jam asked.

"The angels. When they were hunting."

Her skin skittered at the use of that word, Pet's word, but Redemption was right, the work was hunting. Jam tried to imagine Lucille's angels as hunters, remembering how Bitter had told her they'd had to do dark things, hard things. Now they were kindly adults who appeared on TV and came to the schools to give talks. Everyone revered them a little, but no one thought of them as scary, not really. The revolution had ended; there was nothing for them to scare off anymore. Maybe they had been scary during the revolution, though, if they had been like Pet, ripe with that righteous, boiling fire. Jam knew Pet tried not to let her see that fire, so it wouldn't scare her, even though she wasn't its target.

Did you have to be scary in order to be a hunter?

Pet had called her a hunter too, but Jam didn't feel like she had the kind of power to make anyone afraid. She was just a regular kid, not some painted-into-life creature whose entire purpose was literally to catch monsters. She didn't want to fight or be in a new revolution; she was just trying to help her friend in case he was in danger. Once they could get Redemption out and safe, Jam was perfectly fine with running as far away from the monster as possible. That wasn't what a hunter did, and it wouldn't be what the angels would do, but Jam didn't want to be an angel. She just wanted to be herself, the self she was before Pet showed up and started making her look for unseen and unknown things.

"So the obvious monsters would've been like the police and the billionaires," Redemption was saying. "But the angels must have figured out how to find the ones that weren't so obvious."

His curiosity was giving her an idea. *What about the library?*

Redemption laughed. "You just wanna go see Ube, don't you?"

Jam blushed. *Shut up!*

"I'm just saying, that's like your favorite place."

I'm going to hang up on you, Jam threatened, laughing. She did love the library, partly because she loved the books there but also because it was nice to talk to Ube. He'd known Jam since she was a kid, and she came to him often with questions. He'd always answer them, tell her stories attached to the answer, pull out books and send her home with some, and it would always be Jam's favorite part of the day.

"Okay, fine." Redemption grinned, backing off. "We'll go tomorrow and ask your boyfriend."

Jam made a face at him, hiding the relief she felt in her stomach, heavy on the lining. If they looked up criteria, it could be like getting a guide on how to find a hidden monster. She might not even have to convince Redemption, because he'd be right there looking with her, so he'd know how to recognize a monster; he might even tell her everything right away. Then she'd be able to tell him about Pet, and they could figure out what to do next. Jam was still scared, but the library would have some answers, it always did. It would help them know what was unknown. Jam smiled at Redemption.

Thanks, she signed.

Redemption shrugged. "All knowledge is good knowledge. See you tomorrow!"

Jam turned off her tablet after she hung up, then burrowed under her covers and took some deep breaths. She expanded her stomach like a balloon on the inhale and imagined stress leaving from the crown of her head on the exhale. Pet interrupted her by appearing slowly, a heaviness displacing the air.

Well done, little girl, it said in her head.

Jam growled and reached an arm out of her covers, grabbing a pillow and throwing it as hard as she could in its direction. Go away!

She thought she heard Pet chuckle softly before it obliged her by fading into emptiness, leaving a tang of pride in the air behind it.

CHAPTER 7

Jam went down to breakfast in the morning as if the skin of her life was normal, as if it hadn't bubbled and warped and fallen off. Pet was a loud secret in her, a wrong note in the usual harmony of her house, making it discordant, guilty. She could feel the wrongness warbling through the floorboards, and it made her want to finish the hunt quickly, so the secret would no longer be a secret, so everything could return to how it all used to be. Deep inside her, Jam wasn't sure if that was even possible, but she held on to the hope anyway.

"You doing okay, love?" Aloe asked across the breakfast table, and Jam started, her fork clattering against her plate. She'd been so in her head, his voice was a surprise, his concerned face a foreign arrangement of skin and muscle. Her mother was still upstairs.

I'm fine, she signed. She wished he and Bitter would stop asking how she was, if she was mad at them. Their worry felt like a blanket they kept trying to throw over her shoulders, one she kept having to shrug off. They had tried to talk to Jam about Pet, but she didn't want to, and her parents weren't the type of people to force her to open up, so they let her walk away from the conversation each time, and Jam pretended as if she didn't see the synchronized disappointment flashing over both their faces. It built a stone of guilt in her chest, and Jam added it to the pile that had been forming there since she told Pet to stay. The best thing to do was to focus on the hunt and not on her parents or the lies she was telling them with her silence. She ate breakfast quickly, then retreated up to the bathroom to pee and was washing her hands when Pet appeared. Jam felt it gathering in the air before its body showed up, and she watched it appear bit by bit, fur and feathers and horn like dried blood.

Hey, she said.

Pet nodded at her and crouched against the wall next to the shower, its body aggressively eclipsing the rest of the bathroom. It watched her through the mirror, its mouth hanging open, smoke puffing out in short breaths.

How was your night? Jam asked, wondering where it spent the time away from her but not wanting to ask.

Busy. A hunt takes preparation, readying for readiness, it replied.

The bathroom door slid open, and Bitter walked in, tying

a scarf around her head. Jam froze with her hands tangled in a towel, her heartbeat spiking to a blur.

Don't worry, Pet said. She can't see me.

"Morning, sweetness." Bitter dropped a kiss on Jam's forehead and slid the mirror aside to show the shelves behind. "I just looking for my face serum. You seen it?"

Jam shook her head, and Bitter hummed to herself, looking around the bathroom. Jam watched her with wide eyes. There were two bathrooms in that moment, lying on top of each other. One was the room in Bitter's eyes, with the deep tub against one wall, a stack of books lying next to it. The shower, with its patterned tiles and clear doors; the small bottle of serum sitting on a shelf inside. Bitter saw it and let out a pleased "ah!" as she went toward the shower. Jam stared as her mother moved through the second bathroom, the one with Pet in it. Bitter passed through the creature's body as if it was nothing but gold and feathered fog. She touched Jam's cheek and gave her a soft, worried look before leaving with the serum, and Jam sagged with relief as soon as the door slid closed again.

This is too stressful, she told Pet. I just need it to be over.

The hunt takes as long as the hunt takes, it replied. I think you should tell the boy about me.

Jam leaned against the sink and folded her arms. Tell who? Redemption?

Yes. This keeping of a secret, it is not a good thing to keep, you are keeping too many and they do not fit inside your heart, they will keep spaces between you and your humans.

I didn't know you were so concerned about me or my humans.

Pet tilted its chin up. You need the boy to trust you, it said. Secrets do not help trust, do not help the hunt, which needs his trust.

Ah. Jam tightened her mouth. It's the hunt you're worried about. Of course.

It is always the hunt, little girl.

She scuffed the floor with her foot. I don't think we should tell him. It's better if we just stick to the original plan.

Pet shook its head at her. Do you smell your own fears? it asked. They are so strong when they leak from you.

Jam stared at the floor. She hated being accused of fear, of moving with fear. It didn't matter that she really was scared, but she just didn't want to be seen as that, someone who was maybe a coward. Part of why she didn't want to tell Redemption about Pet was because it was scary to think about how he might react, if he'd freak out, if he'd be mad that she hadn't told him earlier. It was even harder to think about telling him why Pet was there and that his house was the beginning, a monster's lair, the starting den. She'd had such a difficult time herself accepting that there could be a monster in his family, how would he take it? But then again, if he was the one being hurt, wouldn't he already know that? Jam imagined Redemption being furious at having a secret discovered, and even just imagining it was painful, because then it would mean that he had a secret that he hadn't shared with her. He couldn't be mad at her for not telling him about Pet, though, in that case. Could one secret cancel out the other?

But also, there was a small chance that Redemption didn't even know he was being hurt. Maybe he thought whatever was happening was okay, maybe the monster had lied that well to him, and she would have to be the one to break the news that none of it should be happening. What if he didn't believe her? What if there was a choice between her and the monster and he called her a liar or said she was being crazy and making the whole Pet thing up, and then he went and chose the monster? What if—

Pet reached out with both its feathered arms and pulled her against its torso. You're spiraling, it said. Just breathe, little girl. Slow and deep, breathe in the air, little human, stop thinking.

Jam closed her eyes, feeling its warm fur through the cotton of her T-shirt, the faint coolness of its goldfeathered arms and the distinct chilliness of her mother's hands stitched to its wrists, a gradation of temperature falling off at the extremities.

Why do you have a pulse? she asked, trying to push the anxiety about Redemption away.

Because I have a body, Pet answered.

So . . . does that mean you have a heart?

Something like that. Not the way you humans talk about the abstract one. But I have an organ that moves fluids around in me.

Blood?

No. My body isn't from this world. I am made of things you have no names for.

Jam nodded. Her own pulse had settled, and the wild-fire beating of wings in her head had calmed down a little. I think I'm okay now, she said.

Pet released her and drew back a foot or two, watching her as she composed herself. Jam looked at her reflection, backdropped by the creature, then wiped her hands over her face. I want to tell him, she said. But I'm scared he won't believe me. About any of it.

I will show myself to him, Pet said. It is hard not to believe me when I am before you.

Jam thought about her parents. I don't know about that, she said.

Your parents are adult humans, Pet replied, pulling on the thought behind the words. Younger ones have fewer blocks about belief.

It was disconcerting when Pet dipped in and out of her head. Jam wondered if it was reading all her thoughts, if that counted as an invasion of privacy.

Pet scoffed. I respect your privacy, it said. I am only in part of your head and only because you humans, your heads are always open. If you are uncomfortable, I can try to ignore your head.

Jam thought about it, then shrugged. I don't mind it so much.

It was actually kind of comforting to have Pet there, like she wasn't alone all the time. You need intimacy to be a unit, and the seamless knowing Pet had of her made up a little for how much she missed the closeness she used to share with her parents.

Don't go into Redemption's head, though, she warned.

Pet angled its face. The hunter only looks into the head of the other hunter, it said. We are connected, little girl. I would not enter the thoughts of any other human.

Oh. Okay. Good.

Tell the boy when you see him today, it continued. I will show myself, and then he will assist us in the hunt.

Jam made a hesitant face. I'm not sure I want to tell him everything, she said.

Everything is many things, Pet replied. What would you like him to know?

Jam twisted her fingers together. It's fine if we show you to him, she said, and we can tell him you're here to hunt a monster, but I don't want him to know it's in his house.

Pet nodded and didn't say anything. Jam wondered what it was thinking, if it thought that leaving out that small piece of information counted as a lie. Maybe her plan was messed up, but Jam hoped that once Redemption got over the shock of seeing Pet, he would be excited about looking for a monster. There was no way that excitement would remain if it became personal, if he knew they were hunting in his house. It was better, for now, if Redemption thought he was saving someone else; everyone's always braver when they think they're the hero. And somewhere along the way, things would click for him and he would realize or recognize what was going on, that the monster was in his house, and Jam wouldn't have to be the one to tell him. It made her chest feel lighter, the thought of avoiding that whole ugly conversation, but doubt whispered through her like smoke seeping under a closed door.

What then? Pet asked. You'll keep that secret forever? You'll never tell him you knew the monster was in his house all along?

Jam smothered the doubt silent. What was important was finding the monster. It didn't matter how, or what pieces of information fell through the cracks in the meantime. All that mattered was making sure Redemption was safe.

Pet cleared its throat. I'm going to go now, it announced. Call for me when the boy is here, when you are ready to tell him your halfway truths.

Jam glared at it, ready to snap a retort, but Pet left before her thoughts could form a shape. The air went empty, and she was alone in the bathroom.

It took Jam all morning to figure out where to reveal Pet to Redemption. Her room was too small; Pet was scarier in cramped spaces if you weren't used to its size. Anywhere outside was too risky, not because anyone else would see Pet but because they'd definitely see Redemption's reaction if he had a bad one. Explaining why her best friend was freaking out at empty air seemed like a conversation Jam didn't want to have with her neighbors. In the end she decided on her mother's studio, because the room was large and Pet looked as if it belonged in there, as much as it could belong anywhere in this world. Bitter was at yoga and Aloe was at work, so she had a little time. Jam went to the studio and looked at the canvas that was still lying on the floor, ripped and empty. Bitter hadn't been painting since Pet showed up. She'd said she needed a break, and both Aloe and Jam understood completely. It must've felt a bit like being betrayed by her own work, Jam thought, to have it come to life and then argue with them, bring stories of monsters in its smoky mouth, awaken a past her parents thought they had escaped. She wouldn't have wanted to paint for a while either if she was Bitter. And maybe the canvas would help to convince Redemption—not that it could tell the story of that night, but perhaps it could help, even looking as it did, just a torn and empty canvas edged in painted smoke. But if Pet stood next to it, the colors would match, right down to the splatters of paint on the floor around the canvas. You could see that they went together. Redemption would look at it, and he would believe.

Jam wasn't even sure what she meant by believe—that Redemption would believe the story she was about to tell him? That he would believe in Pet? It was hard to question its existence once it showed up in all its mighty bulk. Or would he believe in monsters? That felt more unclear. Jam wasn't sure how deeply Redemption bought the Lucille line, that there were no more monsters. She knew he agreed there was a distinction between no more monsters and no free monsters, but she didn't know if he would believe there was a loose monster that needed to be hunted down. Even her parents hadn't believed that, and they knew about monsters, they had grown up with monsters. Jam felt even more sure that her decision not to tell Redemption the monster was in his house was the right move. It was enough to show him

Pet and tell him about the hunt. If they told him too much, he might leave, he might not want to hunt with her, and she and Pet would have a much thinner chance of finding the monster in his house without him.

"I'm doing the right thing," she said aloud into the empty studio, no one there to hear her. The paintings and sculptures said nothing back. Redemption was on his way already. Jam had told him to just meet her in the studio, and he probably thought she was going to show him some of Bitter's work—which was funny, because, in a way, she was. There had been a brief spell when Redemption was interested in painting and had spent a few weeks hanging out with Bitter in the studio. In the end he decided he liked fighting more. It was a shame, Bitter had said; his hands were actually good at making things other than bruises and breaks.

Jam searched for Pet, even though it had told her it wouldn't come until she called. She cast wide through the air the same way she felt through the house, but it all came up empty. It looked like it was just going to be her alone with Redemption, at least at first. That was probably for the best, because once Pet came pouring through nothingness, Redemption's life would change as certainly as Jam's had. It made her nervous—no one outside this house had ever seen Pet. Her family's reality had expanded when Pet was added to it, but everyone else still lived in that other world, the one where creatures from other realms didn't exist. She was bringing Redemption over from that side, colliding the two worlds, and the weight of what she was about to do made the top of her head float away, even as she heard the front door open downstairs and Redemption's voice calling a greeting as he entered. Jam puffed out a hard breath and focused on the soles of her bare feet, pressing them into the wood of the floor, uneven with age and paint and rough varnish. It's going to be okay, she told herself. It's going to be fine.

Part of her wanted to just leave, just run away inside her head, dissociate deeper than anyone could find, but Jam knew she had to stay. The mission needed her. The hunt needed her. She bent over and closed her eyes, taking deep breaths to center herself, and she didn't notice that Redemption had entered the studio until he was taking hold of her shoulders gently. "Jam? You okay?"

Jam straightened herself and tried to inject calm under the skin of her face as she looked at him and nodded. Except Redemption had been her friend for too long, and he could tell when she was pretending.

"I got you," he said, shifting to stand in front of her, toes to toes, his palms still warm against her shoulders. "It's okay. You're here, you're real." He leaned his forehead against hers, and Jam closed her eyes, trying not to cry. He was always so good at taking care of her, and now it felt like her turn to protect him, to do the right thing and make him feel safe, but Jam wasn't sure if she was messing it up already. "It's okay," he said again, and they stood like that for a while, until Jam was settled back into her skin.

She took a deep breath and stepped back a little. *Thanks,* she said.

"Anytime," he replied. "You sure you good?"

Yeah. She smiled to show she was telling the truth this time, then took his hand and led him to the overstuffed orange couch in the corner, under a row of hanging ferns. The two of them pushed aside sketchbooks and worn velvet cushions to make room, then settled down on it. To her surprise, she was eager to tell him what was going on; it had been hard doing all of this without her best friend.

"This is going to sound wild," she warned him.

"I'm ready," he said, his eyes steady and intent. Redemption always loved a good story, the wilder the better. Jam took one of his hands in hers and started telling him everything, from the beginning, from Bitter making the painting and what Aloe had said, about how it wanted to be real, to her sneaking in and cutting herself on the canvas, coming back to find Pet emerging. She watched Redemption's face as she spoke, and it remained the same as it always did, gentle and open and paying attention. He didn't recoil in disbelief when she described Pet. Instead, he leaned forward, his eyebrows pulling together as he listened even harder, as if he didn't want to miss even a fraction of a detail. It had been a long time since Jam had voiced this much or for this long, and she could see that Redemption was taking that seriously. It was entirely possible that he was also thinking she was out of her mind, but at least he was listening. Jam's voice faltered when she told him about Pet's mission, the hunt for a monster in Lucille, and for a second the truth wanted to wing out of her mouth. She clipped it fiercely—now wasn't the time—but she could still feel the faint stone of guilt in her chest as she continued with the story. How could it feel both right and wrong to not tell him the monster was in his house?

"Anyway," she finished, "that's what's been going on. And that's why I wanted us to go to the library today, so we can look up how to figure out what a monster looks like. But Pet wanted me to tell you everything first. I mean, I wanted to tell you too, but I was scared." She shrugged. "Now you know."

Redemption leaned back into the pile of cushions, staring at her wide-eyed. "Whoa," he said. "I wanna ask if you're for real, but I already know you are. So, wow. Just give me a second, yeah?"

Sure, she replied. *It's a lot to think about.*

Redemption threw his hands up. "It's unreal!"

Jam gave a short laugh. *Trust me, I know.*

"I mean, I can't even imagine." He shook his head in awe. "You must have completely freaked out!"

Jam gave him a small smile as a shaky hope built inside her. *You believe me?*

Redemption frowned and sat forward again to take her hand. "Jam, of course I believe you," he said, searching her eyes with his. "You would never lie to me."

Ha, Pet said inside her head, its voice showing up with an abrupt and unbalancing suddenness. He is so confident in you, yes?

Shut up, Jam replied. I didn't call you yet!

Pet ignored her spikiness. You were taking too long. It paused. It's not too late to tell him, you know, it added.

I know, she answered, and she did. Jam had seen it enough times in books and movies, where one person had a chance to be honest, a window of an opening that closed with their silence intact. She knew it would come back and blow up and be worse, all for that window in which something could have been said, and she knew she was, right in that moment, inside that window. Redemption was looking at her with those black, trusting eyes of his, his eyebrows thick and messy above them. Jam could tell him the rest of the message Pet had arrived with—she could tell Redemption all of it, right now—and it would probably be fine. But her friend had believed her so easily, and everything was going so well as it was. Redemption was even talking now, chattering about if Pet was really serious about showing itself, if he was really going to be able to see it. He seemed excited about the whole thing, and Jam couldn't bring herself to break that, the story, the magic of a creature spilling out of a painting. She couldn't contaminate it by involving his house, his family. Pet's version of the story had been breaking her heart since she heard it; she wanted to wait a little before breaking Redemption's.

Am I a terrible person? she asked Pet.

There is no such thing, it replied. There's only what you do.

You know what I mean . . . is what I'm doing terrible? Not telling him?

You humans and your binaries, Pet said. It is not a good thing or a bad thing. It is just a thing.

"Okay, but for real, for real, though," Redemption was saying. "It's going to show up? Right here? Like, right now?"

Jam couldn't help but smile at his enthusiasm. It was so different from her fears. *Yeah, when I call it.*

"Whoa! Okay, okay." Redemption arranged himself on the couch and took a couple of deep breaths to prepare. "And you said it's huge, right? Like massive?"

Yeah, it's pretty big. It might be a little scary, especially because it doesn't have eyes. That takes some getting used to. And the claws. And the horns. And the menacing sense of destruction it tends to drag along with it, she didn't add.

I heard that, Pet said.

Jam almost rolled her eyes. Whatever. Just show up already.

She felt the air start to weigh down in response, and she looked at Redemption. *I'm calling it now, okay?*

"I'm ready," he said, his eyes bright.

Good, Jam said. *It's coming.*

CHAPTER 8

Pet materialized with a bit more style than usual, the air of the studio thickening into a ball of smoke that swelled into a roiling cloud, getting larger and larger until it started to solidify into Pet's shape.

Show-off, Jam said to it, and Pet chuckled back at her. Redemption grabbed her hand and held it tightly, his mouth dropping open as he stared at the smoke. The gray cloud of it disintegrated and drifted away in small streams, leaving Pet's body full and solid in the studio, all gold and red-streaked white.

"Holy shit," Redemption whispered. "It's right there!" He tugged on Jam's hand, then let it go, his head oscillating between her and Pet. "It's right there, Jam!"

Jam's heart was pounding, but his excitement drew a small laugh out of her. *I know,* she said. *I can see it too.*

"I mean, yeah, but . . . wow!" Redemption dragged his

hands down his face in disbelief, muffling his voice. "It's huge!"

Jam laughed again—his reaction was so much like him, that bright, unrestrained wonder. Pet stayed still, as if it knew that moving might be too much in that moment. It was also shielding its simmering menace, hiding it more than usual, and Jam sent it a silent thank-you for that.

Redemption stood up and took a hesitant step toward the creature. "Is this okay?" he asked, turning his head to look back at Jam.

She raised an eyebrow. *It can hear you, you know? Pet's not a thing.*

"Oh shit!" He looked back at Pet. "My bad, I didn't mean to be rude."

"That's fine," Pet said, its voice distorting the air with its not-humanness.

Redemption jumped at the sound, the way the words scraped against reality and echoed inside skin. "Holy shit."

Pet tilted its head, and the horns caught sunlight through the studio's windows. "You say that a lot."

Jam watched Redemption nod way too many times, like he was in a loop or a trance. His eyes were this close to bugging out. "I guess I do, man. I guess I do. Wow. You're real!"

Pet moved its head toward Jam, and she stifled a laugh.

It was radiating layers of exasperation into the air, as if Redemption was an overexcited puppy. Your friend's energy is considerable, it said.

Jam waved a hand, but her friend wasn't even looking at her. "Ay, Redemption," she called out, taking pity on Pet. "You wanna tuck it in a little, maybe?"

Redemption continued to stare at Pet and raised an admonishing finger at her without bothering to turn around. "Leave me alone, Jam! I'm having a moment here."

She raised her hands in defeat and shrugged at Pet. You're just gonna have to deal with it, sorry.

Pet huffed out a large breath of air and watched Redemption as the boy walked around it with greedy eyes.

At least he's not freaking out, Jam said.

I might have preferred that, Pet replied, a trace of a sulk in its voice.

What, you like being feared better?

It has its advantages when you are a thing that does not fit.

Jam didn't have anything to say back to that. It sounded like a sad thing to say, but she wasn't sure if she was reading Pet's emotions properly, or if it could even feel sadness the way she did. She looked back at Redemption, who was muttering to himself and letting out the occasional low, impressed whistle.

"Are you finished yet?" Pet asked after a few minutes, and Redemption jumped, blushing.

"Yeah, sorry." He walked back to Jam and stood next to the couch, shoving his hands in his pockets as his foot tapped excitedly against the floor. "So," he said. "What do we do now? We help you with the hunt?" His eyes shone as they flickered between the other two, and Jam realized that for her best friend, this was a splendid adventure, the kind of thing they'd read about when they were younger, something he could now live out in real life. His brightness swept around the room in a contagious cloud.

Library, Jam said. *Find out how to see monsters.*

"Is Pet coming too?" Redemption asked.

Jam and Pet nodded together, an accidental mirroring.

Redemption frowned, confused. "Um, won't people notice it walking around?"

Don't worry. It can be invisible to other people.

Redemption's mouth fell open again, and he was about to say something, but Jam smacked his arm and gave him a play-it-cool look. He pressed his lips together, but she could feel him suppressing his excitement as they left the house and set out for the library. It was easy for Jam to walk and pretend Pet wasn't walking next to her, because she could still see it with all her other senses; the way it displaced the air, she didn't need her eyes to tell her where it was. The air sang to her just like the walls and floors in her house. Redemption, however, was being incredibly obvious about turning to look at Pet as they walked down the street. Even when he tried not to, his head still swiveled as if tugged by a magnet, inevitably dragging his eyes over.

I think you have to disappear to him, Jam said to Pet. He's just going to keep doing that, and I'm worried someone's going to notice that he's being weird.

He would make a terrible tracker, Pet agreed. Jam felt its presence shift as it concealed itself from Redemption. When the boy looked over again, he gasped to find the air filled with nothing.

"Where did it go?" he asked, leaning close to Jam to whisper the question loudly.

You were being really obvious, she said. *It's giving you some time to get it together.*

"Aw, man. I'm sorry." Redemption looked a little ashamed, and Jam squeezed his arm.

It's okay. It's a pretty big deal to find out about Pet. I'm just glad you aren't scared of it.

He laughed. "I'm totally scared of it, Jam! Who wouldn't be? But it seems to like you, and you're somehow not scared, and that makes me feel like it's okay, you know?"

Jam figured it wasn't a good time to point out that Pet

could still hear everything Redemption was saying—just because you can't see or hear something doesn't mean it can't see or hear you. Maybe that applied to the unseen things Pet was talking about: maybe they were seeing her even when she wasn't looking for them. The thought made the back of Jam's neck prickle with fresh worry. She looked over at Pet, and it was walking the way it always did, slow, full strides, an embodied machine of purpose so strong it had been pulled across worlds. The sight was comforting. There weren't many things Jam knew about Pet, but she knew she would be safe with it, no matter what unseen monsters remained veiled in Lucille.

When they got to the library, Ube was going through a stack of books at his counter. He looked up when they walked in, seeing only Jam and Redemption.

"My favorite researchers," he said, his teeth strong and slightly yellowed, bared in a wide grin. One of his canines had a small gem set into it, catching the light. "What y'all into today?"

Jam tried not to look over at Pet, who was wandering around, looking at the shelves. The library had soaring ceilings and tall windows; it looked like a building made for the creature.

Redemption leaned on the front counter and grinned back at Ube. "We're hunting monsters," he said confidently.

Ube didn't even blink. "Sure thing," he said. "Y'all need supplies?"

"Information," Redemption said. "We're trying to figure out how you'd identify monsters if you wanted to go hunting them."

The librarian nodded thoughtfully. "Which kinds of monsters?"

Redemption glanced at Jam, then back at Ube, uncertainty flickering across his face. "Which kinds?" he echoed.

Ube leaned back and folded his arms. "You gotta know what you hunting when you go hunting for it, boy." Pet looked over from the other end of the room, where it had been reading the spines of a row of books.

He is correct, Pet said in Jam's head. He talks like a human who has gone hunting before.

Jam wondered what Ube had done during the revolution, if he had been old enough then to be involved. He was friends with Bitter, and Jam knew he had been in a wheelchair since he was a kid, so it hadn't been the revolution that put him in it, but that the old world hadn't cared much about people like him. Redemption was asking what the options for monster types were, and Ube was laughing his deep belly laugh, the one that sounded as if it had started at the bottom of a barrel and wound its way up before bursting into the air. Jam tried to imagine a smaller him, if he had that voice then, that laugh. She didn't notice when Pet came up to her until she felt the brush of its presence against her arm.

If the monster is in the house of Redemption, it said, then it is probably a family monster. I know that much.

Jam frowned. A family monster? she asked. You mean, like a private monster?

Pet jerked its chin toward Ube. Tell the man who knows things. He will know which guides to give us.

Jam waved her hand to get Ube's attention, breaking off his conversation with Redemption. Ube leaned forward, his flannel-wrapped elbows on the low counter and his eyes attentive under his thick eyebrows.

"Talk to me, baby girl," he said.

We're looking for family monsters, she signed. When she said that, he frowned and looked at Redemption, then back at Jam, an unfamiliar sharpness taking over his face even as he kept his voice the same, calm and unworried.

"Everything all right with y'all?" he asked. "At home, everything cool?"

His concern made Jam's heart cramp. She wished she could tell him what was going on, and for a moment she considered it. Pet put her mother's stitched hand on her shoulder and squeezed a slight warning.

Do not involve more people than necessary, it said.

But we're just kids, Pet. He's an adult. Maybe he can help.

Or maybe he goes to the house and tells Redemption's parents, Pet countered. *Maybe one of them tells the monster, and it hides even better than it's hiding now. How will we find it then? Your prey should never know you are coming for it, or only when it is trapped and cannot flee and you see it clear and you have it held. Trust me on this, little girl.*

Jam bit down on the inside of her cheek. Why was everything so hard in this hunt? Why couldn't she just pass it off to someone else, have them take care of it?

I know it's difficult, Pet said.

No shit, Jam replied, before smiling at Ube.

We're just doing some research, she signed. *We want to learn more about how things were before.*

Redemption looked confused. Jam had turned away from him slightly so he wouldn't see her sign "family" and "monsters," so he didn't understand where Ube's concern was coming from. "What's going on?" he whispered to Jam, even as Ube relaxed.

"Well," Ube said, his face reverting to its usual lightness, "if it's knowledge y'all want, then you came to the right place."

I'll tell you in a bit, Jam signed back to Redemption as Ube led them into one of the archive rooms. Pet followed, knocking over a row of books with its horns in a moment of careless solidity when it tried to look around too quickly.

Ube stopped and turned, staring at the fallen books for a few beats.

"I wonder if this place is haunted," he said, almost to himself. "Things be acting up." He picked up the books and reshelved them, his hands moving through Pet's body. "But they say that's how it is anywhere you got a mass of knowledge accumulated, so, hey." He shrugged. "Who knows."

Jam nodded in solidarity at the mystery of libraries, then shot Pet a warning glare as soon as Ube turned back around. The creature shrugged and stepped into the room behind them. There was a wall of drawers on the left, each with a small screen displaying information about the drawer's contents. Ube whistled to himself as he tracked his finger down a row of them, read the flickering screens carefully, then pulled three drawers open, reaching into them to pull out thin bundles of paper. He elbowed the drawers closed and turned around with a stack of pamphlets in his hands.

"Come, come," he said, and led them to one of the sprawling wooden tables in the middle of the room. Ube fanned the pamphlets out and then turned to Jam and Redemption, putting some sternness in his voice. "Now, I want y'all to know that y'all's parents may not be too hot about me showing these to you, being as you mad young and whatnot. But all this was material suitable for kids your age back then, feel me? And if you come here looking for information, I'ma give it to you. That's what I do. Ain't no grown-up in the whole of Lucille grown enough to tell you you don't deserve answers to your questions. You understand?"

Jam and Redemption nodded in unison, and Pet cracked its neck behind them.

I like this human, it said to Jam.

"Aight, cool." Ube reached out with his fist and exchanged daps with both of them. "Leave the pamphlets on the tables when you done," he said. "And don't go talking to too many people about this, now, you hear? Most people get real sensitive about monsters." He waited for their nods of agreement before leaving the room, shutting the door firmly behind him. Pet glimmered back into sight for Redemption, who jumped a little in surprise but tamped it down quickly.

"What was all that about before?" he asked Jam.

Nothing, he just got worried when I said monsters, but it's cool. Jam spread the pamphlets out some more on the table, and the three of them bent their heads to look down at the printed pages.

Redemption read the subjects out softly, from right to left. "Dating violence, emotional abuse, drug use . . ."

They're pretty thin, Jam said, interrupting him. *I'm sure we could read through them quickly.* She was nervous about if her plan would work, if anything would come from these old pieces of paper. The best way was to just get it done and see what happened.

"Okay, no problem. Should we split them up?" Redemption asked.

Jam hesitated, thinking quickly. There was a chance her plan wouldn't work if the information she needed Redemption to see, whatever it was, ended up in her pile and not in his. *Nah, I think two sets of eyes are better.*

Pet grunted and wandered off to a corner of the room, pulling open drawers and looking inside.

"What's it doing?" Redemption whispered.

Jam shrugged. *Just being curious?* She pulled half the pamphlets toward her. *I'll start with these and then we switch?*

"Sounds good." Redemption took the other half and settled into one of the chairs.

A silence fell over the room as they read, interrupted only by the gentle rustling of pages turning and the creaking slide of drawers as Pet explored the archive. Jam had started with a pamphlet about parental neglect, and a slow sadness spread through her as she sat flipping through the pages, past the pictures of sad-eyed children and cold grown-ups. She put it down and sighed. *Who would treat their kid this way?*

Redemption shook his head as he dropped his pamphlet on physical abuse and picked up another. He looked slightly sick. "It's really messed up," he agreed. "I can't believe they used to let people get away with this."

But they tried, didn't they? They had child protection services and things like that.

"They didn't try hard enough." Redemption's jaw was set and angry. "No one should be allowed to use their hands this way."

Jam could tell he'd taken that one hard because he was a fighter—someone using that strength and force against a kid was such a violation of how things should be, what hands should do. She reached over and squeezed his arm for a quick moment before they went back to reading, going through a couple more pamphlets each, the late-afternoon light coming through the tall windows.

About fifteen minutes into it, Jam had switched to a booklet about emotional abuse and Redemption was reading one about indicators of child abuse when she heard his breath hiss in a quick intake. She glanced over as he dropped the pamphlet on the wood of the table and stood up, pushing his chair backward.

"Redemption?" Jam put her pamphlet down and got out of her chair slowly, wired with caution. Had the plan worked already—so quickly? She wasn't sure what he had just realized, what might have clicked in his head, but whatever it was, it didn't look good. Pet looked over from the other end of the room and crossed the space between them in three quick steps.

Redemption's face was tight. "I need a minute," he said, raising a hand to keep them away. "I just need a minute."

Jam's stomach dropped. She felt like she had set him up for whatever was happening now. *What is it? What did you read?*

"It's nothing. It might be nothing."

Are you okay?

Redemption didn't answer, and Pet bent its head toward him, taking a soundless step forward, its voice low and echoed and urgent. Jam could almost smell the sweat of the hunt on it.

"You have seen an unseen," it said. "You now know a thing that was unknown. What is it?"

Jam glanced at the pamphlet Redemption had put down. All she wanted was to tell him how sorry she was that she hadn't given him the full warning, that she'd let it blindside him like this. She didn't want to ask him more questions, dig for a truth she was terrified of, try to pull it out of his tongue, but this was a hunt and she had a job to do. *Has someone been hurting you?*

Redemption's eyes flashed at her, blurring with sudden tears. "Not me," he said.

Jam frowned, confused, but Pet reared its head back, light

133

reflecting off the gold. "My instructions were not wrong," it said. "The house of Redemption."

Jam whipped her head around to the creature. Wait, what instructions?

It didn't even look at her. Focus on the hunt, it said. On your friend.

Redemption had turned away from them, walking toward one of the windows, his face in his hands. Jam gave Pet a suspicious look, then followed her friend, stepping in front of him. *You can tell me*, she said.

He laughed, a strange and sorrowful sound. "Maybe I'm wrong," he said. "Maybe I'm making it all up, you know? It could be nothing. Maybe it's nothing."

Frustrated, Jam slid into her voice. "Redemption, what are you talking about?"

His shoulders sagged and he looked out of the window, seeing nothing. "It's not me," he said again, his voice low, almost crawling against the floor of the room. "I think it's Moss."

CHAPTER 9

Redemption wouldn't talk for a while after that. He insisted he needed a little time alone and sat in a corner of the archive room with his head in his hands. Jam and Pet stood at the opposite end of the room, watching him. She hated seeing him this way, shaken and withdrawn; it all felt like her fault.

Don't be silly, Pet said. You didn't put a monster in his house.

I just didn't want this to happen, she replied, wrapping her arms around her body.

Pet shrugged, gold feathers sliding. Who is Moss? it asked.

His little brother.

Ah yes. He too is in the house.

Jam shook her head, staring at Redemption's slumped body. I've never seen him like this, she said.

Knowledge can do that to a person, Pet replied. I've seen

it with you humans. The unseen can tear your eyes open when it comes into sight, and sometimes the mind behind that tears as well.

He's going to be fine, Jam said. She wanted the words to work like a spell, to make the thing true.

We need him to tell us what he knows, Pet answered. Can you make him talk?

Give him a minute, Jam snapped back. She could feel Pet's hunger drumming against the air, against her skin, inside her head. It wanted to hunt so badly that the shield which hid its menace was slipping, putting an edge to its presence.

We're so close, it said. Every minute can matter.

Jam glared at it. Either you wait here, or you go and wait somewhere else, she said. It's not helpful to push him right now.

Pet growled in her head. Fine, it said, go and hold his hand, then. Whatever you humans do.

It stalked away to the shelves. Jam went over to Redemption and sat on the floor next to the chair he was in. She didn't say anything, not wanting to interrupt his silence. Instead, she climbed into the silence with him, staying there, feeling its soft curves. Time beat past them, and Pet simmered in a corner, but Jam ignored it, focusing on Redemption. His breathing was shaky, but when Jam joined him, it steadied a little, and eventually he sat upright, his hands knotted together against his thighs. Jam got up and pulled another chair over.

Talk to me, she said.

Redemption made a face. "I don't even know where to start," he said. "It doesn't make sense."

Jam reached for the pamphlet he'd been reading and looked at the children illustrated on the cover. The paper was almost weightless in her hand. Redemption looked down and took it from her, unfolding it so the pages fell open.

"I didn't think it was anything," he said, his voice loose and wandering. "He's getting older. He doesn't want to be a little kid anymore."

Pet came closer. *What's he talking about?* it asked Jam.

She shushed it impatiently, keeping her eyes on Redemption. He gazed down at the pamphlet, then let it fall, as if his hands had stopped working. It floated to the floor and landed without a sound, lying there as if it hadn't done anything, all angled in its pleats. The silence wrapped around them again, and Redemption kept staring down, at his hands or the floor or the paper, Jam couldn't tell. Eventually she reached out and tilted his chin up with her fingers.

Talk to me, she pleaded.

Redemption's eyes darted away, back and forth, sliding like he was looking for somewhere else to be. "He didn't want me to help him with his baths anymore," he said.

Moss?

Redemption nodded and rubbed his face. "He was fine with it before—fine one day, freaked out the next. Full-on tantrum. My dad came in and couldn't calm him down. We thought he had hurt himself, or the water was too hot or something. Whisper wasn't home. He wouldn't calm down until Mom came in, and then he wouldn't talk about it, not even to her. We thought he was just tired and wanted more attention from her—he's like that sometimes. We didn't think it was anything." Redemption fell silent and twisted his fingers together, pressing and interlocking them over and over. "I didn't think about the bruises," he said, and his voice broke on that last word. "He . . . he's clumsy. We all know he's clumsy." He looked at Jam, his eyes glassing over with tears. "He's clumsy, right?"

Jam fought the surge of heartbreak in her chest. *Yeah, everyone knows he's clumsy,* she said.

"Maybe it's nothing," Redemption said. "Maybe he was just going through a phase, and all the bruises really were from skateboarding."

But you don't really believe that . . .

Redemption's mouth pulled down. "No," he whispered, "not really."

Jam put her hand on his knee and squeezed it so he wouldn't feel so alone.

"I guess I thought something was wrong, deep down," he continued. "I just didn't know what. And some of the things in the pamphlet, some of the things Moss has been saying. I know our parents have been worried too." He shook his head. "None of us knew how to put it together."

Jam controlled her face as he looked at her. "I just want it to be wrong, Jam," he said. "I don't want it to fit this way. It's just an old piece of paper. It's probably wrong. It doesn't know Moss."

Yeah, we don't know, she said.

Pet leaned over from behind her, its shadow falling over both of them. But you can find out, it said.

Jam didn't know what to think. This wasn't what she had expected. She'd been preparing for Redemption to be the monster's target, as much as anyone could prepare for something like that, but hearing that it was Moss somehow made it worse. She hadn't even known it could get worse. Moss was so little, just gaps in his teeth and scabs on his knees and tangled hair and shining eyes. The image of the monster in Jam's head became even darker, the corners of its malice shadowed and sharp. Were there levels of monsters? Were some worse than others? Was that even the kind of thing you could measure?

Do not measure, Pet said in her head. A monster is a monster. A hunt is a hunt. It is simple that way.

Jam let out a breath, and Pet put its hand on her shoulder.

Trust me, it said, the sound of its voice lapping like gentle waves against her mind. Simple is better. Find the monster. Remove the monster.

It sounded like a chant, the way it was distilled, the way it stripped all the mess of the outside down to the bone of the problem. Removing the monster was the best way to protect the people you loved. Seeing Redemption like this was the worst Jam had ever felt in their friendship, especially knowing she'd brought him to the knowledge that did this to him.

All knowledge is good knowledge, Pet said.

I don't know if that's true, Jam thought back. It doesn't feel true right now.

Truth does not care if it feels true or not. It is true nonetheless.

I have to fix this. It's the only way to make it right.

Pet nodded behind her. You are not alone, little girl, and neither is your friend.

The creature was right. Jam leaned forward and put her forehead against Redemption's. They closed their eyes, and she reached for both her voice and the revolution cry they knew and loved so well, hoping he could feel how strongly she was there for him.

"'We are each other's harvest,'" Jam whispered, her voice falling against the skin of his brow, the words like a small rain. Pet made a clicking sound in its chest and leaned in

140

slightly. "'We are each other's business.'" As she spoke, Redemption's breathing began to slow. "'We are each other's magnitude and bond,'" Jam finished. They stayed unmoving for a few minutes, the room silent with sunlight.

Finally Redemption sighed aloud and raised his head to look at her, his eyes reddened. "Thanks, friend," he said.

Jam gave him a tentative smile. He seemed to be holding on to the words, using them as a rope to pull himself into a decision, something that would feel more useful, like he wasn't helpless.

"I want to find out what happened," he said, his face set. "I want to find out *exactly* what happened."

His jaw had become a line of iron, and he was holding his body taut, coiled in a way Jam had never seen before, a great force winding in on itself, building up to spring forward. It wasn't until Redemption stood and looked around for Pet that Jam recognized the emotion he'd finally allowed take hold of him: rage.

Pet loved it. Jam could feel its pleasure vibrating through the air; she could even hear a low but audible purr shaking in its golden throat. Redemption's rage matched the creature's hunger, reflected it almost perfectly. Their combined intent alarmed Jam.

Let's just take a minute, she suggested, but neither of them was looking at her.

"How do we find out who the monster is?" Redemption was asking Pet, his fingers clenching and opening into flashing fists. "What do we do when we find them?"

"We remove them," Pet said. "That is my job."

"Remove them? You mean, kill them?"

Pet tilted its head in pleased amusement and made a chattering sound. "Yes."

Jam shot up to her feet and stepped in between them, waving her arms. "We're not killing anyone!" she burst out, horrified.

Pet was expressionless, and Redemption folded his arms, his eyes glittering.

Come on, man, she said, her hands trembling. This wasn't a cascade she wanted to set off. *We don't even know what's happening. You're talking about a life!*

Redemption looked slightly abashed, but his jaw stayed stubborn. "I can't have someone hurt my brother and nothing happen to them, Jam. You know I can't."

It's not our decision! It's not even Pet's! She shot Pet a stern glare as she said that, and Pet looked back with its nothing face, its claws clicking against each other idly. *We report whatever we find. That's the right way.*

Redemption bit his lip, then nodded. "Fine. Whatever. I just want to know what we're going to do now, like, right now."

"Hunt," Pet replied, and that one syllable shook the air

around them, rolling through it with a deep rumble. Jam could feel how thinly Pet's patience was drawn, how sharp its desire was. She sighed and looked at Redemption.

He picked the pamphlet up from the floor and folded it, shoving it into his back pocket. "We hunt," he agreed.

Jam frowned at him. *You're not going to tell Ube you're taking that out?*

Redemption pushed past her and toward the door. "I don't give a shit about Ube right now," he said. "I've got a monster to find." He left the door swinging open behind him as he walked out.

Pet started purring again, the sound a sharp and scraping vibration. *He's ready,* it said, pleased.

Jam shook her head and arranged the rest of the pamphlets in a neat pile on the table. *I don't have a good feeling about this,* she said.

You shouldn't. There's nothing good about a monster.

She twisted her mouth. *I suppose.*

As they headed out of the archive room, a thought occurred to her, and she looked up at Pet. *It couldn't be one of their parents, could it?*

The question spilled out before Jam thought about what the answer could be. As soon as it was alive, all Jam wanted was for Pet to tell her with certainty that of course it couldn't be one of the parents, of course none of them would hurt their own child. But instead Pet kept walking and didn't reply.

Jam ran ahead and jumped in front of it, blocking its path. I asked you a question, she said. Tell me it can't be one of them.

The creature sighed and looked down at her, its horns bumping into the doorframe. You know I can't do that, little girl.

The answer was too heavy, the possibility crushing. Jam thought about Malachite, Beloved, and Whisper, then hoped desperately that this fear hadn't occurred to Redemption, not yet. It can't be one of them, she said.

Pet pushed her gently out of the way. Monsters can be anyone, it said. We hunt them anyway.

It followed Redemption out of the library, and Jam ran after them, dragging her heavy heart with her. She signed a quick thank-you to Ube as she passed his counter, and he watched as she burst out of the front doors and back into the world.

Out on the street, Redemption was walking quickly, his head down and his hands fisted in his pockets. Pet was walking beside him, one step for three of Redemption's, its head outlined against the sea-blue sky. Jam jogged a little to catch up with them, then fell into place beside her friend.

You going back home? she asked.

"Yeah," he said.

And then what?

She could feel how tense he was, how close to blowing up.

"Then I'll figure out who's been putting their hands on my brother and I'll beat their face in."

Redemption said it like it was nothing, but the anger sat openly on his skin, a new and warbling mask.

Jam glanced at him. "What if it's one of your parents?" she said.

It was one of the fastest mistakes she'd ever made. She'd been determined not to ask that question, to keep that possibility as far away from Redemption as possible, but hearing him talk so openly about the kind of violence he used to reject had hooked it out of her mouth and pulled it into the air. As soon as she voiced it, Jam knew it had been the exact wrong thing to say to him.

Redemption stopped walking and flinched, fresh shock filtering over his face. "What did you just say?" he asked, his voice rising.

Jam felt blood rush to her face. *Forget it, I shouldn't have said it.*

"My parents? You think one of my parents would hurt Moss?"

Her cheeks were hot and itchy. *I don't know, okay?! You said someone's hurting him, I don't know, I thought maybe.*

Redemption still looked horrified. "I mean, yeah, I think someone's hurting him, but not one of my parents!"

Okay, fine! I'm sorry!

They stood looking at each other, a shared cloud of distress knotting around them. Pet had stopped walking when they did and was watching with a patient sort of blankness. Redemption sagged, and the anger he'd been clinging to slipped away, replaced by worry.

"You really think it could be one of them?" He sounded little and scared. Jam wanted nothing more than to take all those feelings away and put him somewhere safe.

I don't know, she answered. *I mean, I don't think so . . .*

Redemption looked like he was about to cry.

Jam turned to Pet. *Could we just stop the hunt for a second?* she asked. *He's not okay.*

Neither is his brother, Pet replied.

Jam stared at it in shock, then the anger showed up. *You know what?* she snapped. *Why don't you just run off and keep hunting if you want. You're so inhuman you don't even see it! I'm going to make sure Redemption's okay, since you clearly don't care about that whatsoever.*

She pushed it out of her mind and turned back to Redemption. *Why don't we go to my house for a little bit?* she said.

Redemption nodded reluctantly, and she took his arm as they started walking down the street again.

We keep getting close, and you keep hesitating, Pet's voice interjected, driving through her skull. This is not how a hunt works, little girl. Your friend's brother could be in danger at this very moment.

If he's in danger now, then he was in danger this morning and yesterday, and every minute since you've been here, Jam pointed out. She tried to keep her face still as she yelled at Pet so Redemption wouldn't notice. Stop trying to rush everything! I don't know much about hunting, but I'm pretty sure that being cautious or thorough matters a lot more than just rampaging in because you want to catch something.

To her surprise, Pet seemed taken aback. It didn't say anything at first but followed behind Jam and Redemption, reeking of contemplation. A block later, it spoke up, its tone grudging.

You are right, little girl, it said. To hunt is to be hungry, but too much hunger can hurt the hunt.

Jam heard the apology under the words. Okay, she said. Glad we're on the same page.

We will soothe your friend before we proceed, Pet

continued. Besides, we need him stable. Agitation like this will only hinder the hunt.

Jam rolled her eyes but didn't say anything, and they walked the rest of the way to her house in silence. The streets of Lucille looked exactly the same; it could have been any other day with the two of them walking home, except for Pet. Jam kept having to reconcile those two worlds: one in which Pet was loud and present, and the other one, the one everyone else saw, where Pet didn't even exist. If she could see and hear and feel Pet, but no one else could, then which world was true? Pet was very clearly here, but those who didn't see or believe in it, all those families who were still living their normal, monsterless lives, they were the majority. Jam looked at their gardens and driveways, still intact even after her and Redemption's worlds had been shaken apart. It didn't seem right.

She and Redemption were stuck in a reality where Moss was bruised and flinching, afraid of his own family, but all these other kids were still there, playing with chalk on the sidewalks and biking down the street and feeling safe in that special way that only Lucille could make you feel. Jam didn't feel safe anymore, and she didn't know if or when she would again. There was a monster here—how was anything supposed to even seem safe again? Especially when none of them had any idea who the monster was. They were probably walking around in plain sight, hidden nicely by smiles and Lucille's optimism. Jam was a whirlpool of anger, sourness, and fear. She couldn't imagine how much worse Redemption felt.

You think your people have let you down, Pet said as it came up beside her. With the things they have believed, they have disappointed you.

Maybe, Jam replied. She had been thinking a little about Aloe, his insistence that Lucille was safe, his resistance toward Pet. Maybe Bitter would have believed Pet more if Aloe hadn't been contaminating everything with his fear.

Don't blame your father, Pet said, interrupting her thoughts. Fear is human. You too were afraid. You too did not want to believe.

It was telling the truth, and that made Jam ashamed of herself. We should've known, she said. It's not that Lucille failed me; it's more like all of us might have failed Moss, you know?

Pet made a small noise between a grunt and a growl. Might, it said. You still want to believe I am wrong.

No, I didn't mean that! She tried to explain herself, not wanting to sound like a coward who didn't want to face the truth, but Pet shook its head.

It does not matter, it said, as long as you are still moving forward. Forward is good. Fear is fine, fear is fearsome. You failed no one—monsters are the ones who do the monster-ing, not you. Also, you are a child.

Jam wanted to argue, but they'd arrived at her house. At the top of the driveway, Pet stopped walking. *I will return when the hunt is resumed,* it said, then disappeared.

Redemption started. "Where did it go?" he asked, looking around.

Not sure, Jam answered. She pushed open the front door, and as they kicked off their shoes, she wondered about the answer. Where did Pet go when it wasn't with her? Surely it couldn't go all the way back to the world it had come out of. Wouldn't it need another painting if it went there and wanted to come back? Or maybe it went to an in-between space, like a waiting room or something.

Bitter came out of the kitchen into the hallway as they were putting their shoes against the wall. "Hello, darlings!" she said, breaking into a smile. "I haven't see you in a while, Redemption. You doing all right? How's the family?"

Jam was impressed with the mask Redemption slid over his face—he did it so quickly that the pain from a moment ago was gone in a flicker. He smiled back at Bitter and kissed her cheek. "I'm doing good, Aunty. They all good."

Bitter hugged Jam and kissed the top of her head. "You looking a little stressed, baby. You tired?"

Redemption gave Jam a warning look, and she almost

rolled her eyes at him. She didn't need anyone telling her to be careful. She'd been keeping Pet a secret for what felt like forever, and her parents hadn't suspected even a sliver of disobedience from her. She knew how to keep things from them.

Little bit, she signed in response to her mother's question.

"You eat yet?"

Jam shook her head, and Bitter clicked her tongue.

"Allyuh does worry me so, I swear. Can't feed yourselves without reminders." She shooed them into the kitchen, where Aloe was frying plantains in slanted golden slices.

Redemption's eyes lit up with glee. "You're making dodo!" It was his favorite food, something Malachite had banned temporarily in their house, because she said it couldn't be good for anyone to eat that much of anything fried for every meal.

Aloe gave an exaggerated sigh when he saw him. "Bitter, you didn't tell me this one was coming. I would have sliced five more plantains, had I known. These ones won't be enough."

Redemption laughed. "It's all right, Uncle. I'm not that hungry."

Aloe held up a hand, the spatula dripping slightly from it. "Abeg. I've heard that before. I still regret that day, my plantain seriously suffered. I think you ate most of them as soon as I removed them from the frying pan."

"Let the man fry more if he want," Bitter said. "It keeps him out of trouble to keep him at the stove." She grinned and winked at her husband, and he blew her a kiss back. Jam and Redemption sat at the table, and Bitter slid them a plate with some dodo on it, the oil draining away on folded paper towels. Jam ground some pink salt over them and nibbled at a caramelized edge, watching Redemption's face in her periphery. He was eating with a casualness that was only a little forced, doing a good job of keeping his mask up. Jam knew how hard it was to stick one to your face around people you didn't have to do that with before. But when realities diverged and you found yourself on a different path from people you used to share a path with . . . well. Masks were useful then; not quite lies, not quite truths. Just decisions about what to be and what to show. Curation.

A loud beep came from upstairs, and Bitter turned her head. "Laundry done," she said. "Jam, you could go up and take out my silk before it start drying? Lie it flat on my bed."

Jam nodded and waited till her mother's attention was diverted to Aloe before leaning in toward Redemption. *You going to be okay?*

I'm fine, he signed at her. *Go.*

He smiled to back up his words, but it had the stretched shine of a mask, and Jam knew it wasn't true. She patted his shoulder as she left the kitchen and took the stairs two at a time, hurrying so she could get back to him quickly. The clothes were a damp mass in the washer, but it was easy to feel out the silk pieces—Bitter's pajamas, a flowered robe, a charcoal slip dress. Jam lay them out on her parents' bed, then started back downstairs, but as soon as she touched the banister, she paused. It was talking to her, as the house always did, but the vibration wasn't making sense. It said Redemption was leaving, which was strange enough, but it was sending hot flashing waves of anger along with it. The front door opened and closed, and Redemption faded away.

Jam ran down to the kitchen. *Where did he go?* she asked as she burst through the door.

Both her parents looked at her, then at each other. "I don't know," said Bitter. "He just storm out so."

"He seemed very upset," Aloe said, frowning.

"Real vex," Bitter agreed.

I'm going to try to call him, she said, backing out of the kitchen as she rummaged in her pocket for her phone. She hit the video call button as she headed for the door, and it rang once before the call got rejected. Jam stared at her phone in disbelief. What was going on?

She opened her front door and stepped outside, looking to see if he was still standing out there somewhere as she recorded a voicenote. Maybe he just didn't want to talk live. "Is everything okay?" she said into her phone. "You just dipped out. What's going on?"

Jam sent the message and walked down her driveway, squinting through the dying day, trying to find him. Her phone buzzed with a reply, a voicenote as well. She held it up to her ear and pressed play.

"You knew it was in my house," Redemption's voice said, partly muffled by the wind, half breathless. He was running, she realized, running away from her as he spoke. "Pet said it . . . in the library . . . it said it didn't make a mistake . . . it said my house . . . you knew it was my house and you didn't tell me." His voice broke off, and it was just the wind and his rushed breaths for a few moments, jagged with anger. "You lied to me, Jam."

The recording broke off, and Jam rushed to send one back. "I'm sorry, Redemption," she said, whispering so her parents wouldn't step out and overhear. "I'm so sorry . . . I didn't want to hurt you, you have to know that, I didn't mean to hurt you." Her hands were shaking, and her finger slipped off the record button, sending the message to him. Jam steadied the screen as the words NOT DELIVERED slid across it. She gasped softly, staring at her phone. For the first time in their friendship, Redemption had blocked her.

CHAPTER 10

Jam couldn't stop staring at her phone. She tried to send more messages, but none of them would go through. This had never happened—no matter how mad she and Redemption were, they always talked about it, they didn't walk away from each other. She held her phone tightly, the glass cold as it dug into her palm. The front door opened behind her, and she heard her mother step out just as Pet condensed in front of her. Jam knew Bitter wouldn't be able to see it, but she didn't turn to look at her mother. She just stood in the driveway, between the creature and her family, her best friend absent in her hand.

"Jam? Everything all right?" Bitter's voice was ridged with concern. "Come back inside."

Jam looked up at Pet. He's gone, she said. He ran away from me.

Pet remained still. What do you want to do? it asked.

I have to go after him. Jam cast her eyes down the street,

looking into the blackness where Redemption's house was buried. *His house isn't safe, Pet. I have to go after him.*

"Is she okay?" Aloe had joined Bitter on the doorstep. "Why is she standing there like that?"

"I think she upset."

Jam took a step away from the house, and Pet took a step toward her, blocking her path.

Do not leave like this, it said. *Your parents will follow. It will muddy the hunt.*

"Jam-jam?" Bitter stepped off the doorstep. "Come inside, nuh."

I have to follow Redemption, Jam said to Pet, her eyes still fixed on the black night, her heart racing. She had to explain; he had to understand.

I will take you to him, Pet promised. *Return to your bedroom, little girl. The boy is needed for the hunt; we will retrieve him.*

Bitter walked over and put her hands on Jam's shoulders. "Sweetness."

Jam jumped, her skin startled.

"You not hearing when I talking to you?"

Sorry, she said. *I was just worried. I don't know why he left like that.*

"It's getting late and you look tired," Aloe said. "Dinner and then bed. You can ask him in the morning."

Bitter steered Jam back into the house, and Pet stayed outside for a few moments, fading only when the door clicked shut.

After dinner, Jam took a shower and obediently went to bed. Her parents stayed downstairs, and she could feel them through the house, the small vibrations as they settled into the couch to watch a film, the whir of the projector, the warmth of the wall receiving the image. She lay on top of her covers in her pajamas for a while, trying to deal with the ache in her chest. She didn't want to look at her phone anymore, to see all the failed messages, the evidence of his rejection, of how she'd broken their friendship. When Pet appeared in the room, Jam didn't get up.

What are you doing, little girl?

Jam shrugged. He doesn't want to see me, she said. What's the point in going over?

So, Pet said, you are afraid again.

Jam sat up, irritation rippling off her skin. Stop saying that!

Stop delaying the hunt, Pet retorted.

Jam folded her arms. I'm not delaying anything, I just don't see the point in going over. Besides, I'm not climbing out of my window, and I can't sneak past the living room.

Pet rippled its fur. I will take you, it said. It is simple.

Jam eyed it. How?

Pet extended one long golden arm, and its fingers un-furled toward Jam. Come, it said.

Jam hesitated. Will it hurt?

Its voice waxed gentle, fingertips light against drumskin. I am not here to hurt you.

You're going to make me disappear with you, aren't you? It will not hurt.

Jam swiveled her legs off the edge of the bed and slid her feet into her slippers, pulling off her bonnet. Okay, but we're just going to try to talk to Redemption, get him back on our side. That's it.

Pet nodded and walked to her, placing one hand on the base of her skull.

Be still, it said, and then the room twisted into a red-and-black circle, and Jam's stomach turned inside out. Her head felt like it was being squeezed, but it didn't hurt. She closed her eyes and tried to fight the nausea, the pressure pushing against all of her body now, against her arms and legs and belly, pressing into her back and shoulders and neck.

It stopped so quickly that Jam had trouble adjusting, her feet tripping over each other and Pet holding her steady. When she felt okay enough to open her eyes, she wasn't standing on hardwood anymore but on thick green carpet that was easy to recognize: it was the top floor of Redemption's house. Jam stared as her slippers sank into it, then her stomach sank as well.

What did you do? You brought me inside the house!

Pet looked down at her. That's where we said we were going, it said. His house.

Yes, but not inside! Jam hissed. How do we explain how we got in?

It does not matter, Pet said. We are here now.

It started moving down the hallway, but Jam stood firm. We can't be here, she said. I need you to take me to the back door or, like, outside his window or something. Just not here.

Pet turned its head, and impatience steamed off it. I am not from this world, little girl, it said, and I am tired of trying to make my ways fit into this one. Come with me or stand there. I can conceal you if you take my hand, but I will not delay this hunt yet again.

It reached out to her, and Jam stared at its blank face, glowing gold in the dimmed lights of Redemption's house. She didn't like it, being here like this, but she couldn't let anyone catch her. Redemption would be even more angry then.

She took Pet's hand and bit her lip. What are we going to do now? Talk to Redemption?

Pet cocked its head to one side, listening. Its feathers chittered, a quick rippling sound. Not yet, it said. We watch.

Wait, so now we're spying on them??

If you wish to call it that. To be still is useful when you want to see unseen things.

This is not okay! Can we just go home? Jam felt like crying. She didn't want to be here, snooping through his house while he wasn't even talking to her. All of it felt wrong.

Pet crouched down in front of her, still holding her hand. Listen, little one, it said. Your friend does not wish to speak to you yet. I can feel how hard that is on your heart, but the hunt must continue. I know it feels bad, but we are only here to help. Hunters must do hard things. I want this to be over for you, but we need to work together to help your friend and his brother.

It put its other hand against her cheek, and the skin was cold. Can you do that? Can you be brave and work with me?

Jam thought about how Bitter had said the angels had to do dark things, hard things, to remove monsters from Lucille. Was this what it had felt like for them? To go against what you usually believed, to betray yourself and the people you loved in small pieces? She sniffed and wiped her eyes.

How do we know we're doing the right thing? she asked.

There is no right thing, Pet replied. There is only the thing that needs to be done.

It watched her as she thought, then made a grudging

concession. You do not have to do this, it said. If it is so wrong in your heart, if you are certain, I can take you home.

Jam sagged with relief, but before she could reply, a door close to them opened and Redemption stepped out in his pajamas. She froze, but Pet tugged at her hand.

He can't see you, it reminded her.

Together they watched as Redemption paused in the hallway, looking down toward his parents' room.

"Come on," he said softly to himself. "You can do this. You got this."

What's he talking about? Jam asked.

I think he is making a decision, Pet replied.

Redemption took a deep breath and smoothed his palms down the cotton of his pajama pants. "Okay," he said. Jam watched as he walked down toward his parents' room and knocked at the door. "Mom?" He pushed their door open and peeked inside. "Dad? Whis?"

He's going to tell them, Jam said.

The bedroom was empty, and Redemption sighed as he looked around, his shoulders drooping. When he turned to head downstairs, Jam and Pet followed, moving through the house like ghosts.

Redemption's parents were in the living room, with music playing and most of the lights dimmed. Beloved had a book laid out in his lap, a circle of brightness cast on it from his reading light. Malachite was dancing alone, her robe billowing in satin gusts, the wine in her glass a red ocean. Whisper sat on the carpet, watching her, their mouth relaxed into a soft smile and their head leaning against Beloved's thigh. Redemption hovered on the outskirts of the picture they made, uncertainty threading through his body.

I don't think it's one of them, Jam whispered in her mind to Pet. I hope not.

Pet remained silent, and Redemption took a tentative half step forward. Then he stopped, shook his head, and tiptoed back upstairs, passing Jam and Pet.

Jam stared after him, confused. I thought he was going to say something to them, she said.

His decision has changed, Pet replied.

Should we do something?

We watch.

Hand in hand, they followed Redemption up the stairs, down the hallway, and around a corner, until they were all standing in front of Moss's bedroom door. It was half open, light falling in a clear path to Moss's bed, highlighting his unconscious face in late-night gold. Redemption looked in, and sadness broke across his face. It took everything in Jam to not reach out and touch his arm, but Pet's hand was locked around hers, and she couldn't spoil the hunt. Redemption didn't want to talk to her anyway.

He stepped into his brother's room, pushing the door almost closed behind him. Jam tried not to think about whether the monster had entered the room like that before, with velvet feet and a secretive heart.

"Hey, Moss." Redemption's voice was soft but firm as he shook his brother's shoulder, waking him up.

"'Demption?" Moss's voice was small and sleepy. "What's going on?"

Redemption lowered his voice, and Jam wanted to step inside as well, crouch invisible next to them and eavesdrop. What was Redemption asking his brother? What was Moss saying? Jam had a sudden moment of wild hope, that Moss would tell Redemption that he was wrong about everything, because then if it wasn't Moss and it wasn't Redemption, then Pet was the mistaken one, and all of this could just slide away.

I am not a mistake, Pet repeated, without turning its head to her.

Jam blushed. I know. I just . . . part of me still wants this not to be real.

Pet nodded, its face directed at Moss's room. I know, it said. It started to enter the room, but Jam pulled it back.

No, she said firmly. Absolutely not.

The creature angled its face at her, horns dark against the slate-gray walls. The identification of the monster is a crucial part of the hunt, little girl.

And Redemption will tell us, afterward. We don't need to listen in on a seven-year-old. It's not right. None of this has been right.

There is no right, there is only the hunt, Pet said, a snarl of impatience behind its words, the smoke from its mouth darkening. They were still holding hands, but Jam squared her shoulders and glared at it.

There is right. Moss is a child. We don't need to be part of this moment.

She looked around, a weed of discomfort growing thick and spiky in her. They hadn't been welcomed into this house, no matter what Pet said, no matter what words it spun about helping and hunts.

We shouldn't be here, she said. Let's go.

She tugged at its hand, but it was like trying to pull a planet. Pet didn't move a fraction.

We are waiting, it said, for the boy to emerge.

We can wait somewhere else, like outside. She pulled harder. Come on, Pet. You said you'd take me out if I said so.

Pet growled, annoyed, but it stepped away from Moss's door. As you wish, it said. We will wait outside.

It slipped its hand to her head again, and the pressure wrapped around her, short and crushing. When Jam opened her eyes, they were outside Redemption's house, sitting on the sidewalk. She let out a shaky breath, and Pet glanced down at her.

Are you well?

She nodded. Thanks for agreeing to leave, she said.

Pet grunted and looked up at the sky. It was a deep blue, studded with stars. Crickets sounded around them, and everything was soft. Jam leaned against Pet's torso and rested her head against the goldfeathered curves of its shoulder, two unseen things in the middle of Lucille.

We wait? she asked.

Yes, little girl. Pet's voice was low and steady. We wait.

Jam woke up with a start, her phone vibrating in the front pocket of her pajama pants. She had a disjointed moment of the sky above her and the trees that lined the street and the sidewalk under her—none of it was familiar, none of it was her bedroom at home. Her cheek was feathered in creases from Pet's shoulder, and her estrogen implant was chilly in her arm. She fumbled for the phone, fishing it out with her half-asleep free hand, hoping it wasn't her parents noticing that she was gone from her bed. Her heart skittered when she saw it was Redemption calling.

She put the phone to her ear, her voice rasped. "Redemption?"

He was sobbing, talking so fast his words were layering on top of each other. "They didn't listen, Jam. I tried to tell them, and they didn't listen."

Jam came alert immediately. "Your parents?"

Redemption hiccuped, his voice clogged. "They didn't believe me, they asked why I would say something like that." He stopped to draw in a ragged breath. "Can I see you?"

Jam turned and looked at his house rising behind her. "Pet brought me outside your house," she said. "We were worried. I can come up."

"I don't know if I can sneak you in."

"It's okay, Pet can bring me right to your room."

There was a brief silence, then a hint of curiosity in Redemption's voice. "Like, it can teleport you?"

"Kinda, yeah."

"Whoa," he said. "Okay."

"See you in a bit." Jam hung up, and Pet looked down at her.

You were right, it said. He reached out.

Jam shrugged. He's my best friend, she explained. He knows I'll be there for him, even after I disappoint him.

Pet nodded and reached for the back of her head, a caress that felt easier each time it happened. The pressure swirled again, her breath caught, and then she landed softly on Redemption's bed. Redemption gasped and recoiled, and Pet let go of her hand and head, backing away into a corner and dropping into a patient crouch.

"That's really weird," Redemption said. His eyes were red and a little swollen, but there was still a touch of wonder in his voice.

Yeah, she signed. *I don't think I'd ever get used to it.*

"I bet," he answered, glancing at Pet. "Thank you for bringing her over."

Pet inclined its head, the horns angling, but kept silent.

Jam tapped Redemption's arm. *Are you okay?*

His face crumpled just a little. "It's been a lot, Jam. Like, I'm trying, but it's been a lot."

She scooted forward to wrap her arms around him, and Redemption held on to her tightly. "It's going to be okay," she whispered.

He has information for the hunt, Pet reminded her, its voice sliding into her head. He knows unknowns. He can see unseens. We need to know and see if we are to hunt and find.

Jam ignored it. "I'm sorry I lied to you," she told Redemption. "I was trying to protect you, but I should have told the truth."

Redemption sniffed. "Yeah, you should have. Like, I get why you did it but . . . still."

"I know. I'm really sorry. I won't ever do anything like that again. I promise."

He nodded and Jam took a deep breath.

"I need to tell you something else," she said. "When Pet brought me over the first time, it took me inside the house by accident. I didn't mean to spy on you, but we saw you go into Moss's room, and then I made Pet take me outside again."

Redemption's mouth fell open. "What? You were in here?"

Jam nodded, her eyes downcast.

"But I didn't see you!"

"Pet can keep me invisible." She was scared to look at his face; it was easier to just stare at the pattern on his duvet cover. "I know we invaded your privacy, and I'm sorry. I'm not handling this hunt thing very well."

Redemption leaned forward and took her hands. "Jam, a creature literally came out of your mom's painting and changed your whole life in, like, minutes. And you had to walk around dealing with all of that by yourself for a while. You're doing your best, and I know you love me and that you're on my team. It's okay." He hugged her, and Jam closed her eyes against the warmth of his neck. Pet glimmered with impatience but kept still, waiting in its corner.

Thanks, she told Redemption after they pulled apart. *Want to tell me what happened with your brother?*

His face dropped. "Yeah," he said slowly. "It's been a shit show."

Jam put a hand on his knee, and Pet inched closer.

"I talked to Moss," he continued. "I told him I figured out that someone had been making him feel bad, and that he didn't have to worry if they told him he couldn't tell anyone, because I had guessed already, so that didn't count. I didn't want to call it a monster, you know, I didn't want to scare him." Jam nodded and kept listening. Redemption folded his hands against his chest, gathering nerve. "He said he wasn't supposed to talk about any of it, or people would get hurt. He was so scared. I asked him if he could write their name or if he wanted to draw a picture."

He loves to draw, Jam said. *That was a good idea.*

"Yeah." Redemption reached over to his bedside drawer and pulled out a folded square of pink paper, handing it to Jam. "He drew this for me."

Pet leaned forward, its throat crackling with static. Jam unfolded the paper and stretched it open between her fingers. She and Pet looked down at it, and she heard a gasp slip out of her mouth, as if it belonged to someone else.

"I showed it to them." Redemption said. "I thought it would be enough."

Jam kept staring at the paper, her fingers numb with shock. It was clumsily drawn, because as good as Moss was, he was still seven—but at the center of the page was an unmistakable sketch of a hibiscus flower.

CHAPTER 11

Jam handed the drawing back to Redemption, speechless with disbelief.

Pet's head tracked the piece of paper. *What does that mean?* it asked Jam silently. *I see that you and the boy understand the symbol.*

It's Hibiscus, she replied. *Their uncle.*

Pet hissed in a long, satisfied breath, but Jam didn't want to talk about the next step of the hunt. This was too much to sit with already.

How could they not believe you? she asked Redemption. *It's right there!*

She didn't say anything about the shock she felt, because she figured it must be much worse for Redemption. Hibiscus was blood, his own family. How could family do something like that?

Redemption folded the drawing back into a square and

put it away. "I didn't think it could be true either, not at first, but . . ." He shook his head. "Moss wouldn't lie."

Did Moss say what happened?

Jam felt wrong asking the question, but even more so when Redemption flinched and looked away.

"I don't want to talk about it," he said, his voice flattened. When he looked back at her, the pain was tamped down into something hammered and hard, locked behind his eyes.

Okay, she said. *Did you tell your parents that part?*

Redemption shook his head. "They didn't wanna listen." He shrugged bitterly. "Didn't seem to be a point."

Jam could see a whole river of things in his face, currents shifting and swelling, vacillating from grief to fury. It must have been devastating for him to find this out, this petaled monster, his trainer, the man he trusted so much, so completely, with his very flesh.

I'm sorry, she said.

"Nah." Redemption's mouth twisted. "Don't feel bad for me, Jam. Wasn't me anything was done to. Was Moss." The hardness in his eyes sharpened. "I'm going to kill Hibiscus," he said.

Pet made a rattling sound deep in its throat, and they both turned—they'd forgotten, briefly and incredibly, that it was there. "We hunt now?" it asked, and it was with a small shock that Jam suddenly noticed the strain the creature was under, ever since they'd identified the monster, the amount of strength it was using to keep still while it waited for them to finish talking. This was what it had come through for, the reason it existed.

Tonight? she asked. *Shouldn't we wait till morning?*

"What's that going to do?" Redemption asked. "Think my parents are gonna believe me more when the sun rises?"

Maybe we can try again.

"They won't listen, Jam! They said the drawing was just a drawing. That monsters aren't real anymore, that I was confusing Moss."

"Humans take too long to see the truth," Pet growled. "I am here because they fail, they have already failed, they will fail some more."

"We should go to his house," Redemption said. "Drag him out of bed, teleport him somewhere where no one will hear him scream."

Your aunt will notice, Jam said automatically. Things felt as if they were accelerating, about to spin out of control.

Redemption jumped off the bed and started pacing as Pet watched him eagerly. "We should draw him out, then. Get him to leave. Get him to come somewhere." He stopped and snapped his fingers. "The training room."

Jam frowned. *That's in the basement. Your parents will be upstairs.*

"Yeah, but it's soundproof, remember? It's quiet, it's isolated. It's perfect."

For a sickening moment, Jam wondered if Hibiscus had ever taken Moss down there. *What are we going to do with him when he gets there?* she asked.

"Allow me," said Pet, but Jam raised her hand at him.

No, she said. *I'm not asking you.*

It made an annoyed snapping sound, and Jam ignored it.

What do you want to do? she asked Redemption.

Her best friend exhaled, his eyes sliding between the cold rage and a younger hurt. "I just wanna talk to him, Jam. I wanna ask him how he could do that. I wanna hear him say he did it. I gotta do something, for Moss." His voice broke on his brother's name.

Jam couldn't argue. It was too big of a hurt, too wild, too incredible to not ask Hibiscus if it was true, why he had done it, why he had become a monster. And then they could figure out what to do, how to get justice for Moss. How to make Hibiscus pay. The anger she felt was something she was leashing as tightly as she could, because it scared her how hot it was, how hungry it was for the things Redemption and Pet wanted—to hurt Hibiscus as much and as senselessly as possible—and maybe only then would any of this start feeling like it made any sense; maybe then the wrongness would ease up a bit.

How do we get him here? It's really late. He'll call your parents.

Redemption smiled a smile that had absolutely no humor in it. "No, he won't," he said. "I'm his fighter." He picked up his phone. "He's not going to call anyone else."

Jam and Pet stared as Redemption called his uncle, a grim light burning behind his eyes. It flared when Hibiscus answered the call. Jam could hear his voice, faint but clear.

"Redemption. Son, you okay?"

Redemption looked Jam straight in the eye as he crumpled his voice with pain. "Uncle Hibiscus," he gasped. "Something bad happened . . . I was training, that new sequence . . . I think I hurt myself real bad."

"You were training this late? And, boy, I told you you not ready for that sequence!"

"I know, Uncle Hibiscus." He hissed in a sharp breath. "I don't wanna tell my parents, they'd kill both of us if they even know you showed it to me, you know how they are. Can you come over? Please?"

"I'm on my way. Don't move too much. Lie down if you can, just breathe. I'ma be over in like ten minutes, okay?"

"Aight, thanks, man."

"You dumb as hell, son. Hang in there." Hibiscus ended the call, and Redemption dropped his mask, his face sliding back into a cold and hurt anger.

"Told you," he said.

Jam blinked, impressed. *Damn.*

Pet unfolded itself and drooled dark smoke out of its mouth. "It is a good trap," it said. "We will wait for the monster to step into it." It reached out its hands to them. "Come," it said.

Redemption stepped back. "Um, I'm good. I can just . . . walk downstairs?"

Yeah, calm down, Jam said to it. We'll just see you down there.

The creature shrugged and vanished, leaving a dizzying space where it used to be.

"That's never going to stop being weird," Redemption muttered, and Jam nodded in agreement. Shoulder to shoulder, they tiptoed down the stairs into the basement, where Redemption's training room had been built. The lights flickered on in a tripped succession once they stepped inside, and Pet was already there, walking around and looking at the equipment. Its feathers flared bright gold when the lights came on. Jam blinked at the glare as Redemption made sure the door was locked behind them.

How's Hibiscus going to get in, then? she asked.

"The outdoor entrance." He pointed across the room to the stairs that led up to another door. "He'll be here any minute now."

It's going to be okay, Jam said.

"Pet, you're going to disappear, right?" Redemption asked.

"Only to him and only at first," it replied.

"Yeah, you're our secret weapon." Redemption grinned. "All he's gonna see are two kids he thinks he doesn't have to be scared of." Pet made a pleased chitter in its chest, its fur ruffling like grass in wind, but Jam was still worried.

We're just gonna talk to him, right?

She was trying not to think about how ridiculous they looked, both in slippers and pajamas, tricking one of Lucille's angels into meeting them in a basement, where they were hiding an invisible creature from another world. This reality was so far outside anything she could've tried to imagine just a few weeks ago.

"It's going to be fine," Redemption said, without answering her question.

Pet growled and turned its face toward the outside entrance as the lock clicked and the door whirred open. Hibiscus came down the stairs in sweats and a hoodie, his sneakers silent against the concrete. He frowned when he saw Jam and walked across the floor, his eyes scanning Redemption's body.

"What's going on?" he said. "You don't look hurt. And, Jam, why are you here?"

Jam folded her arms and kept silent. This was Redemption's house, Redemption's brother to protect, Redemption's monster to fight. She watched Pet out of the corner of her eye, the way it was skulking around Hibiscus, only a few yards out, sniffing, watching, gauging its prey.

"I wanted to talk to you about something," Redemption said. His voice was a little shaky.

Hibiscus stood in front of him, legs wide and irritation in his shoulders. "So you lied to me to get me out here at this time of the night? Shit couldn't wait till morning?"

Redemption's eyes flared. "No," he bit out. "It couldn't."

Hibiscus nodded, clearly pissed. "Aight then, boy. Spit it out. What's got you so riled up that you dragging me out here like this?" Redemption opened his mouth to speak, but Hibiscus held up a hand to silence him. "Actually." He turned to Jam. "Why are you here, Jam? Shouldn't you be in bed? Go on, now."

Jam stared mutely back at him and didn't budge.

"She stays," said Redemption. "I'm the one talking to you."

Hibiscus jerked back at his tone. "Whoa, you better watch that attitude. I don't know what's gotten into you tonight but—"

"How long have you been hurting Moss?" Redemption interrupted.

Hibiscus's words wilted in his mouth, and he stared at his nephew in shock. "What the hell did you just say to me?"

"I said—how long have you been hurting my little brother? You know, your other nephew?"

Hibiscus shook his head. "I don't know what you talking about, boy."

"The bruises, remember? Don't make me say the rest of it, Hibiscus."

His uncle took an automatic step forward, the back of his hand raised at Redemption's insolence, but the boy stepped forward as well, his eyes aflame.

"Do it," he hissed. "Lay a hand on me."

They stared at each other, tension like a whip cracking over and over in the air. Jam backed away slightly, casting her eyes repeatedly at Pet's silent bulk for comfort. The creature was watching intently, coiled with eagerness. I am here, it said into her head. Nothing will happen to either of you.

"What's gotten into you?" Hibiscus murmured. He actually looked sad. "How can you be asking me these things? Who put them in your head?"

"I need you to answer the question," Redemption said.

"Do you have a fever?" Hibiscus frowned and looked closely at Redemption. "Did you hurt yourself for real? Hit your head or something?"

"Don't act like I'm the one anything's wrong with," Redemption said. "You're the one who is a lie, who's been a lie, hiding here for who knows how long. A false angel. A traitor." He spat the word out. "To this family, to Lucille."

Hibiscus expanded with anger. "Don't you ever call me that, boy. Don't you ever accuse me of betraying my position in this community or this family! You don't know the things I've done for both of them."

"What about the things you've done *to* us? What about the things you've done to Moss?" Redemption's voice dropped in disgust. "How can you even look at anyone without shame? How can you look at yourself? At Aunty Glass?"

"Keep my wife's name out of your mouth," Hibiscus growled. His temper was spiking. Jam could almost feel the temperature of the room rise in warning.

"Tell me how long you've been hurting my brother," Redemption replied, never breaking eye contact. Hibiscus stared at him, then made a rough sound in his throat and spat on the floor by Redemption's feet.

"I don't have to listen to this bullshit," he said. "We're done. Find yourself another trainer." He turned to leave, but

Redemption darted around him and blocked his exit. His gaze found his uncle's again, a pin that would not stop piercing. Jam was scared for him but at the same time filled with a bursting pride.

"I said we're done, Redemption."

Redemption smiled grimly. "I see you," he said, calm as the dead, his voice filled with the iron weight of a just pronouncement. "You're the monster, Hibiscus."

CHAPTER 12

The word was like a barbed spear to the man's side. Jam watched as Hibiscus snarled, his face sliding into an unfamiliar hostility.

"Did you just call me a fucking monster?" he spat.

His nephew said nothing, and Hibiscus reached to shove him aside. "Get out of my way, boy."

Redemption shifted his stance, and Hibiscus's hand slid into empty air as Redemption redistributed his weight, just a little but it said enough and it said it loudly. He was prepared to fight his trainer.

Hibiscus recoiled slightly, stunned by Redemption's resistance, even through his anger.

"You serious right now?" he said, squaring his shoulders and tucking his chin. "You really wanna do this, Redemption?"

"You need to admit what you've done," Redemption replied, his jaw solid. "I can't let you leave until you admit what you've done. And you're going to tell my parents, you're going to tell everyone."

Hibiscus laughed, a mocking, grating sound. "I ain't doing shit, boy. Your little brother is confused, that's all. You already tried talking to your parents, didn't you, and what did they all say? That you're acting up, right? Like you got some problem with me and you don't know how to handle it, so you're turning it into this. Ain't nobody listening to y'all kids. This is Lucille. The shit you're talking about doesn't happen anymore, everyone knows that. You can't make it come back just by telling stories when you feel like it." He had a faint smirk on his face, a confidence that made Jam burn with anger.

The next few things happened quite quickly. Redemption hit his uncle in the face, snapping his jaw to the side. Hibiscus didn't even stagger. He turned his head back with a feral smile and clamped one broad hand around Redemption's neck. Jam ran over and grabbed at Hibiscus's arm, trying to pull it down and away.

"Let him go!" she yelled. Hibiscus grabbed her wrist with his other hand and twisted it, and Jam cried out, feeling Pet's presence push through the air at the same time. Hibiscus had only a moment to look up before Pet was on him, and he didn't even have time to scream at the sight of the creature before Pet took hold of him by his rib cage and lifted him up like he was a toy, a rag doll. Hibiscus let go of Redemption and Jam, both of them crumpling to the floor and gasping in pain. Pet opened its mouth and roared, thick smoke sheeting out. It threw Hibiscus against the concrete wall, and his body smacked into it with a dull thud before crashing to the ground. Pet approached him, a low rumble coming from its chest, air vibrating around it. Jam could feel its intent, as clear as a bell, as sharp as a blade. She clutched her wrist to her chest and struggled to her feet.

"Stop," she said, her voice uncertain with fear. "Pet, stop."

It was as if Pet couldn't hear her, couldn't hear anything. This was the culmination of the hunt for it, the final moment, the one it had crossed worlds for. It would not be stopped, but Jam knew she had to try. This was bigger than just one hunt, just one monster. She reached into her head and summoned the loudest silent voice she could find, then threw it as hard as she could in the creature's direction: PET, STOP!

Pet jerked into stillness, then slowly rotated its head toward her. Its blank face had never looked so unnatural, so terrifying. Jam took a step closer to it, her good hand stretched out, the paleness of her palm like a cooling flag, the old bandage still a brown patch across it.

Don't do this, she said to it, just between their two heads, the channel that was theirs alone.

"You were wrong," Pet said aloud. "You have done the

finding, and you have done well, little girl. But you are wrong if you think your people will look. They are cowards. They will not. This is why hunters exist, to see the unseens, to track them down in the shadows they skulk in, to find them. To finish them. Let me do my job."

Hibiscus was still on the floor, his upper body held up by the wall Pet had hurled him into, his front teeth silked red with a bubbled film of blood. He was grimacing in pain, his hand clamped to his side. Redemption had stood up behind Jam, staring at his uncle, his hands balled into bloodless fists.

"Let Pet do his job, Jam," he said.

She turned her head slightly and hissed at him. "Shut up! You're not helping!"

"He hurt Moss! Why are you defending him?"

"I can't argue with both of you at the same time," Jam said through clenched teeth. "Pet, don't kill him. Please."

"You, Jam, begging for the life of a monster, pleading a plea to the hunter." Pet shook its head, and its horns swiveled dark and red. "I was called, and I came. You were called, and you answered. He was hunted, and now he is found. It is well. It is right. It is my right."

"Do it," Redemption whispered, and Jam could hear the tears of rage in his voice. She ignored him. It was Pet she was trying to reach now, Pet with all its menace unfurled, all its great horror released into the air. Hibiscus was staring at it, afraid but proud and silent. He had been a soldier, Jam remembered. He knew he was looking down a corridor painted in his death colors.

"I know it is your right," Jam said. "I know I can't stop you if you don't want to stop. But the town will learn nothing this way, the families will learn nothing. They'll keep pretending all the monsters are gone; they won't remember to look for them. They might not believe us."

Pet flexed her mother's fingers, and its gold claws grew in length, the edge on them blinding. "There can be more monsters," it said. "We will return and hunt them down, one by one, as we have done since time was born."

"But people will get hurt in the meantime! Don't you get it?" Jam's voice was thick with frustration. "You have to give us a chance, Pet; you have to give Lucille a chance to change."

Pet whipped its head around and snarled, an ugly sound, rotten with contempt. "Humans do not change!" it spat. "Look at your precious Lucille, supposed to be purged, supposed to be safe." It flicked a goldfeathered arm in Hibiscus's direction. "Look at this man, this angel of yours. Your angels are monsters, your world is corrupt, and you want a chance? You want me to spare him as an example, as a lesson for the people who forgot how to see, who were careless, and now

185

there is a child who has been hurt and I am come with justice and you want me to stay my judgment in the name of a chance? I shall not, I shall not, little girl. I will cleanse, and when another like him comes, another of me shall come as well, and we will cleanse again."

"Killing doesn't help anything, Pet." She was trying to keep her voice level, but she was shaking so hard. "It doesn't help."

Pet's empty face stayed on her for long seconds. "It is justice," it finally said. "When that child asks, what happened to the man who did this to me, there will be a righteous answer, and it will have been carried out by my righteous hand, and he will at least know that he had justice. He had justice, and the due was done."

"You're so limited," Jam hissed.

Pet made a surprised sound. "I am limited?"

Redemption and Hibiscus were staring at each other in a separate silence. All the air was harsh and electric.

Jam switched to their silent words. *You're only thinking about this one, this child, this monster,* she said. *What about the other children? What about the things we could do to weed out harm before it's done to them? If Hibiscus lives, if the people hear him say what he did, they'll believe him way before they'll believe me or Redemption. They'll know that* they need to look out, to be vigilant. They'll change—they'll watch out for red flags, and it'll be easier to protect those who need protecting.

Pet lifted its chin, about to respond, but Jam put a hand up. I'm not done, she said. I know you don't believe they'll change, but you're wrong. Lucille was made because people changed, because they did something and they wanted to protect others. But you don't want to give us that chance! You don't want to give us a chance to prevent the monsters; you want to wait until the monsters are full-grown and rampaging, so you and the rest of your kind can swoop in and hunt them and save the day. Except that people, kids, are going to get hurt your way. But you don't care, right? As long as you have something to hunt. You don't care if people get hurt. I think that makes you more of the monster.

She folded her arms and stared defiantly at Pet, whose face remained still, trained on hers. Redemption broke the gaze with his uncle to look over at them.

"Is Pet going to do something or what? 'Cos if he won't, I will."

Jam didn't look away from Pet. "You're not going to kill your uncle, Redemption."

"I could!" He took a step forward, and the heavy burning of his anger brushed against Jam's skin. "I could kill him for what he did to Moss. Or I could go to my parents and tell them the rest, the details. Once they hear those, they'd kill him too. If Pet doesn't have the liver to do it."

Jam glanced over at Hibiscus. His face had softened as he heard Redemption talk about killing him.

"My boy . . ." Talking made his ribs hurt, and Jam watched as he doubled over with a groan. Redemption looked unwillingly at him. "My boy," continued Hibiscus. "I'm so sorry—"

"Shut up." Redemption's voice was flint and doors and axes. "I'm not interested in any apologies. You're just sorry you got caught. You're not sorry for anything you did."

Hibiscus teared up, and Jam's memory flipped up the image of him ringside, tears in his eyes, his hand in hers. Her skin crawled.

"I didn't mean to hurt Moss," he said.

Redemption's rage became even more perceptible in the room; it boiled loud and furious. "Don't you ever say his name again!" he yelled. "You don't have a right to say it— don't ever speak it again."

"I just have these feelings," Hibiscus said, his words breaking with emotion. "I need help, my boy. I tried to fight them for so long . . . for so very long. But they were powerful, they took over me . . ." He started weeping then, and Jam stared, disgust sliding around in her stomach. She felt a breeze as Redemption strode past her, past Pet, until he was standing over his uncle. The man lifted a tearstained face to Redemption and reached out a shaky hand. "I just need some help," he said. "I swear I didn't mean to hurt Moss."

The crack of Redemption's fist as it drove into his uncle's face was the loudest thing Jam thought she had ever heard. Hibiscus sagged immediately, unconscious, and Redemption massaged his hand as he looked back up at Jam and Pet.

"So," he said, "what are we going to do with him?"

They both stared at him, the echo of bone against bone fading from the room.

"I need a decision," Redemption said. "My parents will notice I'm not upstairs soon."

Jam looked at Pet. "Please," she said. "There has to be another way."

Pet growled in its throat, an unhappy sound. "Very well, little girl," it bit out. "You have such faith in your people, I will chance it this once."

Jam felt tension drop out of her bones. "You won't kill him?" she asked.

"He might wish I had," Pet said grimly, "but no, I won't kill him."

"So what's going to happen to him instead, then?" Redemption asked. "He's just going to deny everything as soon as the grown-ups ask. He'll say Moss is making it up. And I don't want them questioning my brother. He shouldn't have to defend himself. He's only seven, Jam. He shouldn't have to."

"He won't," Pet said. It looked around the training room and jerked its head toward some of the equipment. "Bring that over here."

Redemption dragged the bench over and levered half of it so it was at a right angle, a narrow L. Pet lifted Hibiscus easily with one hand and deposited him in the seat. "Tie him in," it said, so they did. "Step away."

Jam took Redemption's hand as they pulled back. "What's it doing?" Redemption whispered.

"I don't know," she said. Pet looked like it was concentrating. It leaned down and breathed a faint yellow smoke over Hibiscus's face. The man choked and coughed as soon as he inhaled it, coming back to consciousness with reddened eyes.

"What are you doing, Pet?" Jam asked. The creature paced slowly in front of Hibiscus, casting an ominous shadow over his body.

"I am going to make sure that he tells the truth to the rest of your humans," Pet replied.

"Oh yeah?" Redemption scoffed. "Good luck with that."

Pet turned its head to him. "You should not mock, little boy. You have no idea what I am or what I can do." It said these words calmly, without apparent malice, but there was so much danger steaming off its body that it landed in the air as a threat, and the blood left Redemption's face.

"You can't force him to tell them the truth," Jam said.

Pet's face tracked toward her, and she felt a sheen of an emotion coming off it, not quite regret but something bittersweet. "I need both of you to close your eyes and cover your faces with your hands. Look away. Make sure you do not look back."

"What's going on, Pet?" Jam was alarmed now.

"Look away, little girl."

Redemption turned and covered his eyes. His fascination with Pet was overshadowed easily by his fear of Pet's power, of the death chafing just inside it. Jam was not afraid; she refused to be afraid.

"Tell me what you're going to do," she said. "I won't look away until you tell me."

The gold feathers started lifting off Pet's arms, metal flowing through the air as if it was water, a massive unfurling. Jam's eyes hurt watching it, they were so bright, and they seemed to grow in intensity as they lifted off. The skin that had been covered by the feathers was furred like the rest of Pet, slicked down and wet. Jam stared at the ripple of rising feathers coming off its arms, and all at once, all of a sudden, she saw that the feathers were wings, that Pet had been wrapped in wings, down its arms, over its shoulders, masking its face. And now it was opening its wings, and there was a great light starting to seep out from under the shield of gold feathers, and Jam knew as surely as if Pet had told her itself that it was going to show its true face to Hibiscus. She didn't know what that would look like, what it would mean, or what it would do to Hibiscus, but somehow she knew that it was a terrible thing that was about to happen. Pet's wings came off its shoulders and neck, and light poured down its throat, piercing in strength.

I will be blinded, Jam thought. If I don't look away, I will be blinded.

Images of the angels from those old books flashed through her head, and she looked at Pet one last time, while she could, at the hands she knew so well, the torso it had comforted her against, the horns she was no longer afraid of, these new wings loud with righteousness. She reached for it in her head.

I know what you are, she said.

For a moment she thought she saw its mouth stretch into a smile thick with smoke, fractures of light breaking through.

DO NOT BE AFRAID, Pet replied, and then it turned to Hibiscus and the rest of its wings snapped out into fullness.

Jam whirled around just in time, throwing herself on the ground and covering her face, squeezing her eyes shut.

The light that burst around her was so bright that it pushed through her hands and eyelids, and all she could see was a massive blankness edged in a darkness so deep it felt like she had been pulled out of her world entirely and cast somewhere else. She could hear Hibiscus screaming, his voice warped and bending as it went on and on, scraping his throat. The walls and floor of the training room were trembling; Jam could feel it bucking under her body. She curled up tighter and hoped Redemption was okay.

Hibiscus's screaming went on for minutes after the light faded away, and Jam could feel that Pet had left, that the air held a strong emptiness where its body had been. She didn't move for a while, keeping her hands pressed to her face and her body against the rubber floor. Bright shapes and colors flooded behind her eyelids, ghosts of Pet's light. Jam was afraid to open her eyes in case she couldn't see, it had been so much; it felt like it had stabbed through everything, and Jam didn't see how she could be the same once she stood up, if she stood up. So she lay there until gentle hands touched her shoulder.

"Jam?" Redemption's voice was low and worried. Hibiscus had stopped screaming. "Are you okay, Jam?"

She slowly let her hands fall away and opened her eyes, blinking as they readjusted. Redemption was kneeling next to her, fear frantic on his face. He hugged her tightly.

"I was so scared something happened to you," he said, his voice muffled against her hair.

"I'm okay," she whispered. She sounded raspy, as if she'd been screaming with Hibiscus, who was moaning softly in his corner of the training room.

Jam and Redemption looked at each other, both afraid to see what Pet had done. Redemption tightened his jaw.

"Come on," he said, standing up and holding his hand out to her. "The room isn't built to block that level of sound, and the whole house shook. They're going to come down."

Jam nodded and took his hand, pulling herself up. They kept holding hands as they edged slowly toward Hibiscus, dread bubbling in their chests. He was limp against the wall and floor, his head hanging down and turned to one side. Redemption nudged one of Hibiscus's outstretched legs with his foot, and the man moaned again but didn't move.

"What did Pet do?" Redemption asked. "And where did he go?"

"I don't know." She walked around Hibiscus's body and crouched down beside him.

"Be careful, Jam."

"Don't worry, he can't do anything." Not after all that screaming, she thought. No one could do anything after screaming like that. Screaming like that meant you had been broken, completely shattered and crushed, and there was no

194

way you were a threat after that. There was no way you were even whoever you had been before, not after that. Not after seeing Pet's true face.

She poked Hibiscus's arm, and he groaned, rolling his head up and toward them. Both Jam and Redemption screamed and scrambled backward, Jam falling on her butt and still pushing back and away, away from the burned, boiling holes where Hibiscus's eyes used to be, from the scalded tracks where the redblack ran down his cheeks into his wet and weeping mouth.

"I'm sorry," he babbled, "I'm so sorry, I'll tell them everything, I swear, I'm so sorry."

Jam was crying, her palms hard on the floor. She could hear Redemption throwing up behind her, the convulsions of his guts and throat as they emptied him in horror.

"I'll tell them everything, please don't let it come back, Jam. Jam, are you there? Redemption? I'm sorry, y'all, I'm so, so sorry." Hibiscus broke down into open sobs, and Jam covered her mouth with a hand. They could all hear voices and doors as people came downstairs, and Jam felt the familiar vibrations of her parents' footsteps, even through the rubber of the training room floor. They must have noticed that her bed was empty and had come looking for her.

She wanted to move, but she couldn't, not even to check on Redemption, not even to turn her head away from the vengeance Pet had unleashed on Hibiscus's face. She was still there when the grown-ups came into the room, when Glass screamed and ran to her blinded husband, when Aloe cursed at the scene, his voice rough and explicit as he picked Jam up and cradled her to his chest, even as tall as she'd gotten. She saw Bitter's face slide in front of hers and heard her mother's voice twisted with concern, heard Beloved and Malachite and Whisper overlap each other as they rushed to Redemption, one of them sending another to make sure Moss didn't enter the room. Hibiscus sobbed louder when he heard the little boy's name.

"What happened?" Glass asked, her voice shrill with panic. "What happened to him?"

Aloe was already carrying Jam out of the room, and she could feel the arrow of his heart pointed toward their house, toward home. He was single-minded, cutting through the air before him.

Bitter walked beside him, her hand on Jam's arm, her voice low and soothing: "We be home soon, doux-doux. You eh have to worry. We be home soon."

Behind them Jam could hear Hibiscus's voice, ragged and pleading, saying how he would tell them everything, everything, if they could just please make sure it didn't come back for him.

EPILOGUE

Pet didn't come back that night, or the next one, or the next.

There was a hearing after everything, after Hibiscus's confession was heard. Aloe and Bitter didn't want Jam to go, but she'd been a witness, so she had to. It was hard to see everybody, to see how desperately Redemption's parents held on to Moss, fluttering and fussing over him, none of them looking as if they'd slept in days, which they probably hadn't. Redemption looked drawn and exhausted when he sat down next to her, and their hands found each other, no words needed. Jam's parents sat beside her, and Redemption's parents sat beside him, Moss squeezed in between them, their hands brushing over him repeatedly, as if they needed reminding that he was real or he needed reminding that they were sorry—for not protecting him better, for not seeing or stopping what Hibiscus had become. All the parents leaned over the children as they exchanged soft words and softer touches, hands gripping hands, palms cupping cheeks and jaws, all heavy with sorrow and regret.

The whole of Lucille showed up for the hearing, spilling in crowds outside on the lawn when the building couldn't accommodate them, watching the outdoor projections of the indoor proceedings. When Glass gave her testimony, it nearly drove Malachite mad.

"I didn't want to believe it," Glass said. "I thought . . . I thought he was better." A shocked murmur ran through the crowd as she looked up, straight at Malachite, who was bloodless with building rage. "I'm so sorry, Mal. He was so good with Redemption, it had been decades, you have to understand, it had been decades . . . he had been so good. I didn't want to believe he would again . . . not with Moss . . . not with our little Moss . . ." She had been twisting a hand-kerchief in her hands, and she brought it to her face as she broke down into tears.

Malachite let out a guttural scream and launched herself out of her seat, aiming with violent hands for her sister. The room broke into tumult as Whisper threw a forearm around Malachite's stomach, pulling her back. "I'm going to kill you!" Malachite screamed at Glass. "You knew! You knew and you let him near my babies, you monster!" Whisper put their other arm around her and locked her against their body while Beloved held Moss to his chest, shielding the boy's ears and head with his large hands. Redemption stared at his mother and his aunt, tears dripping down his motionless face, his hand a vise crushing Jam's. She didn't mind. Bitter stretched an arm around both Jam and Redemption, holding them as close and as tight as she could.

Aloe was standing, furious, gesticulating toward Glass as he shouted: "Get her out of here! Can't you see what she's doing to the boy's family? Are your heads not correct?!"

They ended the hearing early that day. It took another week for Lucille's angels to come to a resolution: how to rehabilitate Hibiscus and Glass, what amends they would have to make, what the city would have to change so this didn't happen again. Most of the angels had walked around like ghosts the whole time, shocked to their core at what Hibiscus had done. His confession left no room for doubt or questioning; he had been open with all the details of what he had done, desperate even to share them. It had been hard for the other angels to hear it, to see one of their own confess to being something else, something other, something ugly. It shook the whole of Lucille, what had happened with Hibiscus. The angels launched new investigations, new policies and programs meant to fix the blind spots they'd created by claiming that the monsters were gone. In some ways the hunt had returned to their city, but no one argued with them. "We do not know if there are more monsters in Lucille," the angels said, "but we intend to find out, with your help. We intend to help those who need helping, whether they are harming or harmed. We are each other's harvest, we are each other's business."

Lucille had responded as one. *"WE ARE EACH OTHER'S MAGNITUDE AND BOND."*

Jam and Redemption had given their testimony in private, just to the angels, who had exchanged meaningful looks that no one would explain before letting them go. No one had mentioned Pet since.

When Jam asked Bitter why, one night when her mother was tucking her in, Bitter paused and looked around before answering in a low whisper: "I not suppose to tell you this, but the angels of Lucille, they know about creatures like Pet. From time of the revolution."

Like the first one you brought through? Jam asked. *Was that during the revolution?*

Something drifted behind Bitter's eyes. "That was a long time ago, sweetness. Is another story altogether." She smiled and the thing behind her eyes fled with her smile.

I think Pet was an angel, Jam said.

Her mother looked at her studiously. "Is possible," she said.

I mean a real angel.

"I know what you mean, child. Angels could look like many things."

So can monsters.

Bitter's face grew sad. "Yes, doux-doux. I know."

She sat with Jam for a little bit afterward, then kissed her goodnight and turned off the lights as she left. Jam felt the air change as soon as she was alone, become heavier and stifled with presence.

She sat up in her bed excitedly, casting out in her head. Pet?

I am here, little girl.

Jam could see it now, huge in the dimness of her room, glinting gold and glowing splattered white. Where have you been? she asked.

Away. Must still be away, but came to see you, my seeing one.

Jam felt tears start up, and she dashed her hands against her eyes. She was so tired of crying. You're here to say goodbye, aren't you?

Yes, little girl.

She could see now that its wings were enclosing its body once more. I'm going to miss you, she said.

Pet rested a hand on her knee, the gold claws digging slightly through her sheets. And I, you. It was an honor to hunt in this world beside you.

Are you an angel? Jam asked. Or just a hunter?

Pet crouched by her bed, its horns outlined in the window behind it. Is an angel not always a hunter, is a hunter not always an angel? it replied. As long as the target is a monster.

Will there be more monsters? Jam asked. Pet stayed silent, its face blank, and she tried to explain more. I'm scared. You're leaving, and I'm scared.

Do you remember the last thing I said to you before tonight? it asked, and Jam nodded. Put faith in that, little girl.

Jam nodded again, and Pet leaned its face in toward hers, touching their foreheads together. She could feel the heat of its true face pushing through the gold feathers, warming the skin of her forehead. I must depart, Pet said. Tell me the words so I know you will remember them, you will hold on to them and it will be as though you are holding on to me, and you will not forget, yes?

I won't forget.

Pet nodded. Tell me, it said again.

Jam stared at the locked layers of Pet's face and remembered how it looked that night, with its mighty wings outspread, terrible justice come to Lucille. What would have happened to Moss if she had not believed Pet, if she had refused to look at the unseen things? She took a deep breath and smiled shakily at Pet, knowing this was the last time she'd ever see it.

Do not be afraid, she said.

A gold mouth smiled, and smoke dripped out.

Good, Pet whispered, and then it was gone and Jam was alone with the house, with the whispers in the floorboards and her parents asleep in their room, one last tendril of smoke fading before her eyes.

ACKNOWLEDGMENTS

This book would not exist without Chris Myers. Back in 2016, he asked me to write a young adult novel and I refused, saying I had another list of books I needed to finish writing first. A year later, I gave him thirty pages of what would become *Pet*, and a few months after that, the first draft was done. Thank you, Chris, for believing in this work as fervently as you do, for advocating it into existence, for caring so much about young readers and what worlds they need. It's an honor to work alongside you.

Thanks to my sister, Yagazie, for being my favorite beta reader and live-texting me her responses as she went through the manuscript. I'm always excited to share these stories with you.

Massive thanks to the team at Make Me a World, to the force that is Barbara Marcus, and to my phenomenal agents at Wylie, particularly Jacqueline Ko and Alba Ziegler-Bailey.

To my lovebears and squad, you are brilliant, and I'm so grateful you're in my life.

To my readers, thank you for receiving this work, engaging with it, and sharing it! I want *Pet* to reach as many readers as non-humanly possible, so it can do the work it's meant to do in the world. We are each other.

With all my love, thank you.